The story, all names, characters, and incidents portrayed in this production are fictitious. No identification with actual persons (living or deceased) is intended or should be inferred.

First paperback edition: May 2025

Book cover by DreamStudio AI Generator

ISBN   978-1-9680271-2-4 (6x9 paperback)
ISBN   978-1-9680272-0-9 (6x9 hardback)

The Survivor's Compound

Part I
Thirteen Days In

M.P. Hendy

Table of Contents

Chapter 1

A Lesson in Manliness

David stood in the middle of his living room, staring out one of the French doors overlooking his property. It had been two days since he ordered the power to be cut off. Every generator, every solar panel, anything that could be a conduit, was cut off. The steel core shutters that blocked his windows and French doors were opened this morning. Revealing a world on the brink of collapse. A world still in denial of the hell it would soon find itself.

His wives, children, and other family members waited for his next order. Tiffany, Jennifer and Summer, his blonde core trio, teased each other relentlessly. Elena, couldn't be bothered to change out of pajama pants. His younger wives, Taylor, Nicole, and Kayla, all seem to adapt quickly without social media. Jessica, his favorite and most possessive wife, was suffering from TikTok withdrawals. Meanwhile, his newest wife, Tanya and her younger sister Seo-Yeon, humbled themselves, thankful for David's intervention.

Aidan, his oldest son and his wife Alissa, kept themselves busy, checking the wiring and troubleshooting the generators. Brian, without his computer or video games, continued to maintain the garden in the lower bunker with his mother, Jennifer. David Jr., seemingly immune to such worldly things, kept himself busy, training the twins and patrolling the property with Kyle, Kayla's younger brother. Lily, his eldest daughter and her husband Josh, seem to be spending a lot of time rehearsing the Renado breeding program. Finally, the twins, Seth and Grace, were trying out their best 'creepy twin' moments.

"Alright everyone, it's been two days and as I promised, we're going to turn the lights back on. At least, I hope we will." Elena looked at Aidan with a concerned expression, they weren't used to David showing any doubt. "David, is everything okay? I've never actually heard you doubt yourself before," Elena said hesitantly. David shrugged. "It's just that, Electricity was a rare commodity the last time, and I'm certainly no expert. That's why I was redundant with everything," he finished.

Aidan and Alissa stood up. "You two, go downstairs and power up the generators. Brian, you go too. Once they close the circuit, watch for any thrown breakers. Once you're done, and everything is good, let us know on these," he said, handing over two hand radios. As the three went downstairs, Kayla approached. "Are you worried something might happen?" David shook his head. "I'm not, but I know better than to get my hopes up. Besides, this house is the evil lovechild of redundancy and overkill.

"Honestly, the grid would have probably been fine with just powering them off, but we have at least three levels of redundancy for everything." "Hey David?" Kyle sauntered over. "What do you mean redundancy?" David was getting ready to explain when the radio keyed. "Dad, Generator's on and the breakers are good, try the lights," Aidan said, obviously speaking too close to the microphone. As David reached out to turn on the light… they unceremoniously turned on. No dramatic flair, no sparks flying, just a simple click. "Good job guys, now take Kyle and go to the apartments next," he said, dropping his arm. "Voila!"

Jessica ran to the garage to check the phones and tablets in the faraday cage, a formation of women behind her. "As I was saying. Three redundancies. We have backups for our backups and triple level protection for everything," David said before handing Kyle a radio. As Jessica returned with her phone, Aidan, Alissa and Brian followed close behind. "The phone works, but there's no service!" Jessica whined. David didn't respond, he just kissed her on the cheek before stopping Brian. "Brian, see if you can get that network antenna working, okay?" David whispered. Brian nodded before heading to his room.

As Aidan and Alissa put on their gun belts, Jennifer, Kayla and Nicole returned from the garage, phones and tablets in hand. "Master, there's no network access. Is that because of the blackout?" Jennifer asked, a sad look in her eyes. David smiled, taking her hand. "It's probably safe to assume the network won't be up and running for a long, long time," he said as he kissed her cheek. "David, take Kayla, Taylor and Josh. Go check the perimeter. I want an assessment on all the cameras, sensors and trip wires," David barked. Little David responded with a prompt salute, eliciting a giggle from Jennifer.

Tiffany returned, already halfway into her boots. "I'm going to check the barn, I miss my little marshmallows," she said, grabbing her gun belt. David closed the distance in two long steps, taking Tiffany in his arms. "Darling, do you know how sexy you look in jeans and a pistol?" he asked, growling theatrically in her ear. Jessica cleared her throat. "Ahem!" she said, obviously calling out their public display of affection. "I thought you were going to check the barn?" she asked, her voice flat. Tiffany, wearing a blush that crept up her neck, quickly regained her composure. "Right. Barn. Lily's coming with me." She said as she practically dragged Lily out the door.

Once safely inside the barn, surrounded by the comforting aroma of hay and bovine bliss, Lily finally broke the silence. "Tiffany, can I ask you something...personal?" Tiffany, already knee-deep in miniature cattle, looked up, a slight frown creasing her brow. "Of course, honey. What's on your mind?" Lily hesitated, kicking at a stray piece of straw. "It's about Josh...and...well...sex."

Tiffany choked slightly, nearly swallowing her gum. "Sex? With Josh? What about it?" "It's...okay. Fine. But...Dad is...well, Dad. He...knows things." Lily blushed crimson. "I just...I think Josh could be...better." Tiffany burst out laughing. "Oh, honey. You have no idea what you're asking." "What do you mean?" Lily asked, confused. "Your father, Lily, is a freak of nature. Nine women and we still can't keep up with him. He's got stamina that would make a marathon runner weep." Tiffany paused, considering her words. "He's a Dominant, Lily. He likes control. But he's also incredibly receptive. He pays attention. He's...passionate."

Lily stared, wide-eyed. "Passionate? Josh is...nice. He brings me flowers." "Nice is good, honey. But nice doesn't necessarily set your bedroom on fire." Tiffany chuckled, then grew serious. "Look, your father is...gifted, in certain areas. He's gentle with Taylor, Nicole and Tanya. Treats them like porcelain dolls. He's...forceful with me, Jennifer, Elena, Summer and Jessica. We like it that way. It's not a one-size-fits-all kind of thing. It's about connection, about understanding what your partner needs." "So, what am I supposed to do?" Lily asked, her voice small.

Tiffany thought for a moment, stroking the head of a particularly fluffy miniature Hereford. "Tell you what. Instead of me giving you a lecture on the birds and the bees, I've got a better idea. Have Josh hang around your dad for a few days. Shadow him. Observe him. See what he does, how he acts, how he listens. David might not consciously teach him, but Josh will pick up on things. Subtleties. It's like osmosis, only with more testosterone and carefully concealed BDSM gear." "BDSM gear?" Lily squeaked.

Tiffany waved her hand dismissively. "Don't worry about that. Just focus on the shadowing. And Lily?" "Yes Ma'am?" "Remind Josh that your father is a soldier, unusually strong, and has a very low tolerance for disrespect. He might be your dad, but he's still Master to a lot of people in this house. Josh needs to be respectful." Lily swallowed hard. "Okay, Tiffany. I will."

Back at the house, little David, Kayla, Taylor and Josh were strapping on their gear in the gun room. David, as always, was a picture of calm efficiency, double-checking every strap and buckle. Kayla fussed over the placement of her knife, Taylor meticulously tightened her body armor, and Josh...Josh looked utterly terrified.

"Alright, sunshine," David said, clapping Josh on the shoulder, "let's go make sure our little slice of paradise is still here. Kayla, you're on point. Taylor, you're on rear guard. Josh, stick with me and try not to trip over your feet. And remember, not everything's a threat, so let us know." As they headed out, David noticed Josh's wide-eyed expression. "Something wrong, son?" he asked, his voice deceptively gentle. Josh gulped. "No, sir. Just...a little nervous." David gave him a knowing look. "Nervousness is healthy. It keeps you sharp. Just remember, keep your eyes open, keep your head up, and communicate."

As they patrolled the perimeter, David would periodically stop and point out subtle details: a broken branch, a faint footprint, the way the wind rustled through the trees. He explained how to read the land, how to anticipate threats, how to use the environment to their advantage. Josh, initially overwhelmed, slowly began to absorb the information, his initial fear replaced by a growing sense of focus.

Back at the house, Tiffany watched them walk away, a thoughtful expression on her face. "Well, Lily," she murmured to herself, "let's see if we can turn your nice, flower-bringing husband into something a little more...interesting." She glanced back at the barn. "And maybe, just maybe, it'll give David a run for his money."

The perimeter check with Taylor, Kyle, and little David had been… enlightening. Mostly, it had been a masterclass in coordinated efficiency, punctuated by Kyle's colorful commentary and little David's unnerving accuracy with his pistol. Josh, meanwhile, felt like a clumsy extra in an action movie.

David settled into one of the porch swings, its gentle creaks the only sound besides the chirping of cicadas. He gestured for Josh to take a seat in a nearby rocking chair. Homer, Rahab, and Judas, the trio of dachshunds, immediately arranged themselves around David's feet, their long bodies forming a furry barricade. "So," David began, his voice calm and even, "how did you think it went?"

Josh swallowed, feeling the weight of David's gaze. "I… I learned a lot. Taylor's really good with the dogs, Kyle's got an eye for detail, and little David… well, he's a prodigy." David chuckled, a low rumble in his chest. "They've had years of practice, Josh. You're just getting started. Lily tells me she wants you to…" he paused, searching for the right words, "…absorb some of my… assertiveness."

Josh winced. "Yeah, that's… that's the word she used." He knew he wasn't exactly the picture of masculine dominance. Back on the farm, he was the quiet, dependable one. Here, surrounded by David's capable wives, his hyper-competent children, and even the damn dachshunds, he felt… inadequate.

David leaned forward, his expression softening. "Look, Josh, I wasn't always this…" he gestured vaguely at himself, "…this person. When I was younger, I was skinny, weak. Easy prey. I got bullied a lot." Josh looked up, surprised. He couldn't imagine David ever being anything less than the composed, capable man he was now. "My father," David continued, his voice tinged with a hint of bitterness, "he didn't teach me how to fight. He taught me how to be afraid. I never learned how to lead, how to stand up for myself, or for others."

He paused, staring out at the valley. "It wasn't until later, much later, that I learned those things. I joined the military. I found... a wife, had three sons. Learned discipline, leadership. Picked up a couple of foreign languages. Became proficient with weapons, even got a few college degrees." "You mean... before the... blackout?" Josh asked hesitantly.

David nodded. "Way before. I learned how to fight. I learned the value of taking care of people. But it was never enough." He sighed, a weary sound. "My wife... nothing I did was ever good enough, she didn't trust me. She couldn't see the man I was trying to become. Then she divorced me."

He looked back at Josh, his eyes filled with a deep, unsettling sadness. "Then, after a few short relationships that never panned out, I met someone. Someone I truly loved, someone who could see right through me. Someone that loved me for who I was, Samantha. But she was... damaged. Too damaged to let anyone close. She could never accept me." He shook his head. "I lost all hope for happiness."

Josh felt a lump forming in his throat. He wasn't sure what to say. "So, I became a security contractor," David continued, his voice regaining its composure. "Good pay, dangerous work. Then the blackout happened. My children...

10

they were killed, because they weren't trusted to protect their mother or themselves. My mother died. Even Samantha… she couldn't cope. She ended it all."

David's gaze hardened. "Seven years, Josh. Seven years of surviving all this." He gestured, as if referring to the world. "Seven years of fighting. Of killing. I killed to protect the innocent. I killed to punish the wicked. And sometimes, I even killed to put the dying out of their misery." He stopped, the swing falling silent. The only sound was the buzzing of insects in the nearby fields. "Then," he said softly, "then I regressed. Forty years. I still don't know why. Back to being thirteen years old. But with all my education, all my experience, all my strength, and unfortunately… all my guilt, trauma, and pain."

Josh stared at him, his mind reeling. He knew David had mentioned something about remembering the future, but he hadn't truly grasped the weight of it. "Only this time," David said, a glimmer of something like determination in his eyes, "I knew where my choices led. I knew what the future held. I cultivated my strength. I built on that foundation. I built this." He gestured to the house, the property, everything. "I refused to make the same mistakes; I refused to be the victim."

He paused, taking a deep breath. "You see, Josh, you remind me of my children. The ones that never got a fair chance. That's why I'm telling you all this." Josh's head spun. He felt like he was standing on the edge of a precipice, about to fall into an abyss of revelations. "But… Lily…" David nodded. "Lily sees potential in you. She sees kindness, loyalty,

11

and a good heart. She wants you to be stronger, more assertive. And I want that for you too. You can't build an empire on pride or selfishness. We're similar, but I had to do this twice to get it right. You... have me to help you."

He leaned closer, his voice dropping to a quiet whisper. "There's something else you should know, Josh. Something that might explain a few things." He fixed Josh with a knowing look. "My ex-wife... the one who didn't trust me? That was Lynn. Your mother." Josh's jaw dropped. "What?" David held up a hand, silencing him. "And Samantha, the one I truly loved, the one who couldn't accept me? That was Jessica, after trauma damaged her."

Josh was speechless, struggling to process the information. His wife's stepmother was David's lost love, and his mother was David's ex-wife? It was like some bizarre, twisted soap opera. David wasn't finished. "And the last person I killed out of mercy, Josh? The one I ended their suffering before the apocalypse destroyed them completely?" He paused, his voice thick with emotion. "That was Tanya."

Josh stared at David, his mind completely blank. Tanya, the soft-spoken, gentle esthetician, the woman who always had a kind word and a soothing touch, was... killed by David in his previous life? David reached out and placed a hand on Josh's shoulder, his grip firm. "I never married Lynn in this life, Josh. But she took my kids from me, not just figuratively, but literally. I married Jessica before her trauma could reach her. And I saved Tanya before the apocalypse destroyed her."

He looked at Josh, his eyes filled with an intensity that both frightened and fascinated him. "You have the determination, and you have Lily. But you have something I never did. You have a family here that will support you, this entire family… is your family. This ranch… is your home." As David spoke, Josh's heart began to race. "Kyle and David can make any weapon you want and train you to be lethal with it. Everyone here has a skill you can learn from. So, take advantage of that."

The information overload was staggering. Josh felt like he'd been hit by a truck, a truck carrying the weight of David's past lives and existential paradoxes. He stammered, "So… Lynn… is your ex-wife? My mom?" David nodded, his gaze steady. "Yes, in my last go-round. And before you ask, no, I didn't intentionally seek out your mother in this timeline. Fate, or whatever you want to call it, has a morbid sense of humor."

Lily, who had been observing the conversation with rapt attention, piped up. "See, Josh? Dad avoids drama, but drama just loves him!" She punctuated her statement with a playful shove to Josh's shoulder. A wave of nausea washed over Josh. This was too much, too fast. He looked from David's intensely serious face to Lily's strangely supportive one. He needed air. "Uh… I need to… mulch some tomatoes," Josh mumbled, backing away slowly. "Yeah, the tomatoes are really suffering." He turned and bolted towards the barn, leaving David and Lily in his wake.

Lily sighed dramatically. "He's going to need a lot more than shadowing to become assertive," she said, shaking her head. "But I still want him to learn from you, Daddy." David chuckled, a deep rumble in his chest. "He'll get there, his heart's in the right place, he just needs a purpose. And you, my dear, need to learn the delicate art of being a wife. Not just a warrior, not just a strategist, but a wife." He clapped his hands together. "Let's start with Tiffany. She's the backbone of this family, the nurturer. Learn from her, Lily. Learn how to build a home, not just defend a fortress."

Meanwhile, Josh was not mulching tomatoes. He was hiding in the barn, hyperventilating in front of a miniature Dexter cow named Praline. "Okay, okay," he muttered to Praline, "Mom is David's ex-wife. Jessica is Samantha. I'm dating the daughter of a time-traveling paramilitary genius who's lived through the apocalypse. And my mother is... somewhere. Probably trying to ground me for the blackout."

Suddenly, the barn doors swung open with a theatrical flourish. Alissa stood there, a mischievous look in her eyes. "Hiding from reality again, Josh?" Josh groaned. "It's all just... so much. My mom, David's past, Lily wanting me to be more... David." Alissa sauntered over, leaning against Praline's stall. "Lily sees something in you, Josh. Something good. Something worth... sharpening." She winked. "Besides, you're way too cute to waste on being a doormat."

Josh blushed. Alissa's candid behavior always caught him off guard. "And you're not weirded out by any of this?" "Weirded out?" Alissa laughed. "Honey, my aunt is my father in law's wife. Weird is practically in my bloodline. Plus," she added, lowering her voice, "Aidan is kind of cute. Time-traveling future knowledge and all." "Alissa!" Josh exclaimed, scandalized. "What? I'm just saying! Anyways, don't let Lily boss you around too much. Just... be a good guy. And maybe learn to stand up for yourself, just a little bit." She patted his arm reassuringly. "Now, come on. Jennifer made brownies. Chocolate. with walnuts."

Josh's stomach rumbled. Brownies did sound good. He took a deep breath and straightened his shoulders. Maybe, just maybe, he could navigate this bizarre new reality. With the help of brownies, Alissa's questionable advice, and, against his better judgment, David's... mentorship.

Later that afternoon, as the sun began its descent, David sitting on a bench, facing the sunset, took a sip of his coffee. "David. Can I talk to you?" Josh asked, a weary expression on his face. "Sure Josh, grab a seat, I could use the company anyway," David said, pointing to an empty chair. Josh took a deep breath before continuing. "I understand why you didn't go after mom again. I mean, she is a lot to handle. But... Why did you kill Tanya?"

"Why do you want to know, Josh?" David asked, his voice a low rumble, his usual jovial demeanor vanished. He set his half-empty mug down with a soft clink. Josh rubbed his hands together, a nervous gesture. "It's just... I see the way she treats you, the way you treat her. It's...remarkable. I want to understand what you thought in that moment. Before...back then." David sighed, running a hand over his head. "I understand your curiosity, but it's not just my story, it's hers as well. It wouldn't be right to reveal her past... or future... or whatever the hell this is."

Almost as if on cue, Tanya glided through the French doors leading to the dining room, a plate of cheese and crackers in her hands. "I heard part of your conversation. What about my past?" she asked, tilting her head. She leaned down, placing a kiss on David's cheek as she set the plate beside him. David reached up and took Tanya's hand, gently pulling her down onto his lap. "He wants to know why I killed you."

Tanya's eyes widened for a fraction of a second, then relaxed. "Oh, I see," she said, almost dismissively. She nestled closer to David, resting her head against his chest. "Tell him everything," she said, a strangely satisfied smile playing on her lips. David looked at Josh, his expression unreadable. He took a deep breath. "It started that blistering morning on the bus, seven years in... It's the story she told me..." He paused, gathering himself. "How she fell into sex work. How the world collapsed around her. It evolved from a story of hardship to one of pure terror."

He continued, relaying the horrors Tanya had described. "She was used as a commodity. Traded for a can of food for thirty minutes of...comfort. Sold, bartered, used as bait. Luring the desperate into a false sense of security." David's voice hardened. "Hygiene and medicine were luxuries. Her body became a breeding ground for infection, disease. She knew she was as good as dead. Anyone stupid enough to take advantage deserved what they got." He paused again, letting the weight of his words hang in the air.

Tanya picked up the narrative, her voice surprisingly even. "Then I met David. His presence...it was strange. A calm, yet a terrifying rage at the same time. I knew what to expect. But instead of using me, he fed me." A faint smile touched her lips. "I slept that night like I hadn't slept in years, while he kept watch. When we prepared to leave I wanted to cry, I wanted to thank him, but doing so would hurt him," she said softly. "Then he promised to take me away from my suffering. Just the calm and the promise in his voice was the best thing I had experienced in nearly a decade. I remember closing my eyes, trying to picture David, a man I had only just met, carrying me in his arms. Then suddenly, everything went dark." "I beheaded her," David said, coldly.

"I knew what I was doing," David said, his gaze fixed on some distant point beyond the road. "It wasn't mercy, not entirely. It was… pragmatic." He paused, searching for the right words, something that rarely happened. His autism, usually a source of meticulous detail and unwavering focus, felt like a burden in this moment, amplifying the weight of the memory. "She was a walking biohazard. Letting her live would have endangered everyone. But it wasn't just that. It was...seeing the look in her eyes. The complete and utter lack of hope. The acceptance of a fate no one should ever have to endure."

He looked down at Tanya, her face serene as she nestled against him. "She didn't ask for it. She didn't beg. She simply...accepted. And that, I think, is what made the decision for me." Josh swallowed hard. "But...beheading her? Why?" David's expression hardened. "Quick. Clean. As painless as possible. A bullet could have attracted unwanted attention, a knife might have caused unnecessary suffering. I knew my skills. I knew what I could do to make it as swift and dignified as possible, under the circumstances."

He looked at Tanya, a flicker of something akin to apology in his steel-blue eyes. "I offered her a clean end, a release from the horror she was living." Tanya reached up and caressed David's face. "He's right, Josh. It was the best thing anyone could have done for me. And...," she paused, an adoring look in her eyes, "it worked out pretty well, didn't it? I got a second chance."

Josh ran a hand through his hair, overwhelmed. He'd expected a story of hardship, perhaps a tale of rescue and redemption. He hadn't anticipated this raw, brutal honesty, this unflinching acceptance of a past that seemed almost impossible to comprehend.

Lily walked in, holding Homer, Rahab and Judas by their leashes. "Hey everyone, I'm taking the pups for a walk." Lily gave Josh and Tanya a curious look. "What's going on?" "Just listening to a story," Josh replied, trying to sound casual. Lily tilted her head. "Oh? One of Dad's stories? Those can get pretty intense." She looked at David, her brow furrowed with concern. "You okay, Dad?" David offered her a reassuring smile. "Just sharing some...history, Lily-bug. Nothing to worry about." Lily, ever perceptive, didn't look entirely convinced, but she didn't press the issue. "Alright. Well, I'll be back in a bit. Josh, you coming?"

Josh hesitated. He wanted to escape, to process everything he'd just heard. But he also knew that this was exactly the kind of situation he needed to learn from, to become the kind of leader David was. "Yeah, I'll come," he said, standing up. "Just…give me a minute."

He turned back to David, his voice barely a whisper. "I…I don't know what to say. Thank you for sharing that." David nodded, his expression unreadable. "There are things you need to understand, Josh. Things you need to be prepared for. The world isn't always pretty. Sometimes, it's a dark, ugly place. And sometimes, you have to make difficult choices. Choices that will haunt you for the rest of your life."

Chapter 2

The Renado Madness

The gentle hum of the generators, vibrated against the pool wall, creating an endless, subtle agitation to the water. Inside, the scene was far removed from the escalating chaos above ground. Artificial sunlight streamed from the UVB lights, reflecting off the shimmering surface of the pool. Tropical music played softly, adding to the surreal atmosphere. Kayla, strategically positioned behind a portable cabana, expertly mixed a vibrant blue concoction.

Jennifer, resplendent in her nakedness, raised her glass, "To new beginnings! And to never being ashamed of who we are!" A chorus of "Cheers!" echoed around the pool as everyone took a sip. Lily, perched nervously on the edge, glanced toward the closed door. "Are you sure my dad won't let the boys in?" Jennifer flashed a mischievous grin. "Honey, your dad promised. He knows better than to interrupt a sacred female bonding ritual. Besides," she added with a wink, "he's got his hands full keeping them busy. Imagine Josh's face if he knew what he was missing."

Lily giggled, then took a tentative step into the water. The initial shock of the cool water against her skin made her gasp, but the warmth soon followed, melting away some of her anxiety. Tiffany, enjoying the moment of respite, floated serenely in the middle of the pool. Her long blonde hair fanned out around her. "Relax, Lily-bug. Just let go. Jennifer's right, we all need this. It's not every day the world falls apart and you get to skinny dip with your mother and... well, the entire Renado sorority chapter."

Nicole and Tanya, still clinging to the edge of the pool, exchanged hesitant glances. Tanya, her dark hair cascading down her back, chewed her lip. "I just... I don't usually do this kind of thing." "That's the point, sweetie," Jennifer said, gliding towards them. She took Tanya's hand and gently pulled her into the water. "No judgments here. Just acceptance and a little bit of chaos."

As the music swelled, Jennifer began to dance, her movements fluid and uninhibited. She beckoned the others to join her. Elena, needed no further encouragement. She moved with a confident swagger, her long black hair swaying with each step. Soon, even the initially reluctant Nicole and Tanya were swaying awkwardly, giggling nervously. Over at the bar, Kayla was in her element. Mixing drinks was her passion, and doing it naked only added to the fun. Jessica, sprawled on a lounger, raised her empty glass. "Another blue lagoon, please! And make it strong!" Kayla winked. "Coming right up, sassy-pants."

Summer, watching Lily from across the pool, who still struggled with seeing her daughter as a woman, remembered changing Lily's diapers just yesterday. But seeing the hesitant smile on Lily's face as she splashed with Alissa reassured her. Perhaps Jennifer was right. Maybe this was exactly what Lily needed.

21

Without warning, Jennifer grabbed Tiffany and pulled her into a deep kiss. Tiffany, after a moment of surprised laughter, reciprocated with gusto. Then, Jennifer moved on, planting a lingering kiss on Elena, a playful peck on Summer, and a lingering, sensual kiss on Jessica. Some of the women blushed, some giggled, but everyone seemed to enjoy the uninhibited expression of affection and acceptance.

Meanwhile, outside the fortified walls of David's house, the men were indeed occupied. Aidan, with his custom, propane-powered hotrod grumbled as he and Josh rode on patrol. "I'd rather be inside with Alissa." Josh grumbled, "I just want to spend time with my wife, but she's having some team building conference with the ladies." Aidan sighed, "Probably baking cookies." Brian, Seth, and Grace patrolled the perimeter fence, their expressions serious. Meanwhile, Kyle and little David, were carefully reloading ammunition. Kyle, ever the professional, inspected each round with meticulous care.

Inside the house, David waited. He knew what Jennifer planned. She insisted that nudity inspired confidence and confident women inspired assertive men, something that both Lily and Josh needed. Besides, he liked knowing they still had the freedom to enjoy themselves.

Back in the pool, Jennifer surveyed the scene with satisfaction. The women were laughing, splashing, and embracing. Even Tanya and Nicole were starting to relax, their inhibitions melting away with each sip of the tropical cocktails. Lily was actually dancing, a genuine smile lighting up her face.

The aroma of David's signature post-swim lunch — a surprisingly delicate chicken salad with mandarin oranges and toasted almonds — filled the house. Aidan, Josh, Kyle, little David, Seth, Grace, and Brian sat around the gargantuan dining room table, a mismatched band of brothers and in-laws, picking at their food.

A wave of coolness washed over the room as the women began to trickle in from the recreational bunker. Jennifer, her blonde bob, damp and clinging to her face, was first, followed by Tiffany, Summer, Alissa, Seo-Yeon, Nicole, Elena, Taylor, Lily, Jessica, Kayla and Tanya, each wearing their swimsuit, a towel draped carelessly over their shoulders, and an air of relaxed contentment.

The men's jaws, particularly Josh, Kyle, Aidan, and Brian, threatened to detach completely. It wasn't just the sight of twelve stunning women in various states of undress; it was the casual, unrestrained affection that followed. Jennifer, with a playful wink at the assembled group, strode directly to David, wrapped her arms around his neck, and planted a noisy kiss on his cheek. "Master, that pool was perfect," she purred, her voice a seductive whisper that sent shivers down Brian's spine.

Before anyone could process that, Tiffany pulled David's ear and thanked him for "another perfect de-stressor." Summer murmured something about Jennifer, and Elena, never one to be outdone, kissed him lingeringly on the lips, whispering a suggestive comment about inviting him next time. Even Nicole, usually reserved, pressed a tender kiss to his temple. Jessica, however, simply bypassed the entire buffet of affection. "Daddy," she announced, plopping herself directly onto David's lap, her legs dangling over his, wrapping her arms around his neck. "Mine," she declared with a mischievous grin. "I'm not moving." Kyle choked on his chicken salad.

Aidan, though used to his father's... unique family situation, couldn't help but raise an eyebrow at Alissa, who shamelessly leaned over and gave Aidan a long, lingering kiss. "Best son ever," she said, before snagging a roll and winking. Lily, not to be left out, mirrored the affection, latching onto Josh's arm with a giggle. "Did you see the way I did that?!" she whispered loudly, before nuzzling into his ear, "I'm learning so much from everyone!" Josh, still slightly shell-shocked, just managed a weak smile and a nod. Seo-Yeon, bless her heart, hesitated, offering Brian a tentative smile, a delicate blush blossoming on her cheeks. Brian, usually quick witted, was rendered speechless.

The women, oblivious (or perhaps deliberately so) to the male consternation, chatted amongst themselves about the water temperature, Kayla's concoctions, and Jennifer's shameless behavior. They helped themselves to the chicken salad, their movements fluid and coordinated, like a well-oiled machine. The men, meanwhile, sat in stunned silence, forks suspended mid-air. Little David, ever the pragmatist, simply shrugged and continued eating. Seth and Grace, the twins, exchanged knowing glances, a hint of amusement flickering in their eyes. They'd seen it all before. Probably even had a spreadsheet about it somewhere.

David, observing the chaos with a faint smile playing on his lips, finally cleared his throat. He recognized the subtle signs of feminine conspiracy, the unspoken plans for an afternoon dedicated to… well, he preferred not to dwell on the specifics. Suffice it to say, it involved scented candles, questionable massage techniques, and a whole lot of giggling. "Alright, ladies," he announced, his voice carrying a note of gentle authority. "I think these guys deserve the rest of the day off. Just make sure the house doesn't burn down."

Josh, finally finding his voice, stammered, "Mr. David, sir? What… what am I going to do the rest of the day?" he asked, still struggling to understand David. Lily, squeezing his arm, leaned close and whispered in his ear, her breath warm against his skin. "Me," she breathed, her eyes sparkling with mischief. Josh's face turned the color of a ripe tomato. He swallowed hard, his carefully constructed facade of assertive manhood crumbling around him like a poorly built sandcastle. He glanced nervously at David, who simply raised an eyebrow and gave him a knowing smirk. "Just… try to keep up, Josh," David said, his voice laced with amusement.

Meanwhile, Lily, buzzing with the residual energy of the pool party and several alcoholic beverages, pulled Josh's hand. "Come on, honey," she slurred slightly, tugging him towards their room. As they disappeared down the hallway, Josh, who had been patrolling all day, felt a surge of frustration. He was tired of the charade, tired of feeling inadequate. He knew Lily's intentions were good, but the constant comparisons to David, the subtle suggestions, were grating on him. When they reached their guest room, a different kind of fire ignited within him.

He turned to Lily, her platinum hair still slightly damp, her eyes sparkling. Instead of his usual tentative approach, he grabbed her, pulling her close with a surprising force. His kiss was demanding, his hands roaming with a newfound urgency. Lily gasped, initially surprised, then her eyes widened with pleasure. The pent-up frustration, the desire to prove himself, had unleashed a raw, untamed passion in Josh that Lily had never seen before. In a moment, he had taken control, leading her into a world of fierce, uninhibited pleasure, setting her body ablaze with agonizing lust.

Back in the dining room, emboldened by the combined effects of alcohol and blatant encouragement, Seo-Yeon, with a nervous giggle, reached for Brian's hand. It was an innocent gesture, or so it seemed. She gently took his hand and pressed it, palm down, against her thigh. The innocent façade crumbled the moment his finger twitched. A barely perceptible movement, a subtle glide of his knuckle against her swimsuit-clad labia. Seo-Yeon gasped, a tiny whimper escaping her lips.

Brian, paralyzed by a mixture of shock, exhilaration, and the sudden realization that he was potentially violating every social norm he'd ever been taught, froze. He looked at Seo-Yeon, his eyes wide with a silent question. Seo-Yeon, despite her initial boldness, was still incredibly shy. The apocalypse hadn't magically erased her inherent nature. But she did want Brian. She wanted to experience intimacy, the kind she'd only read about in romance novels, with someone who had always been genuinely kind to her. Someone who, even before the world went dark, had made her feel seen and appreciated. This was her chance, a chance to shed her inhibitions and embrace the chaotic freedom of their new reality.

And Brian? Brian was more than willing. His wide eyes softened. He looked from Seo-Yeon to Jennifer and then to Tanya. Both women wore matching predatory grins. He looked to David for help, but David, ever the enigma, was calmly eating his chicken salad. He brought his eyes back to Seo-Yeon, his thumb gave another slight twitch. Seo-Yeon gave him a mischievous smile and stared into his eyes.

Leaning closer, Seo-Yeon whispered in Korean, her voice barely audible above the soft clatter of silverware, "naneun neoege naleul jugo sip-eo" – "I want to give myself to you." Brian, bless his heart, just blinked. Thanks to his father, he was fluent in Arabic and Spanish. He even managed to learn Mandarin, but Korean was not on the curriculum. The passionate declaration was completely lost on him, leaving him utterly clueless. He gave her a confused, yet hopeful, look.

Seeing the communication breakdown, little David, perched beside his older brother, stifled a giggle. Leave it to Brian to get caught up in a moment he didn't even fully understand. He leaned in conspiratorially, his voice a low murmur in Brian's ear, delivering the message in perfect, fluent Arabic, knowing Brian's fluency. "ruh biha 'iilaa altaabiq alsuflii waijealha aimra'atan." He punctuated the instruction with a playful nudge. "Take her downstairs and make a woman out of her."

Brian's eyes widened again, this time with understanding, and a healthy dose of panic. He glanced at his mom, Jennifer, who simply winked, a devilish twinkle in her eyes. Great. No help there. He looked back at Seo-Yeon, whose shy smile was now radiating pure anticipation. "Downstairs?" Brian stammered, his voice cracking slightly. "Now?" Seo-Yeon just nodded, her cheeks flushed a delightful shade of pink. With a sudden surge of courage, she stood, pulling Brian up with her. He stumbled slightly, nearly knocking over his chair, but managed to regain his balance. "Uh, okay," he mumbled, letting Seo-Yeon lead him towards the hallway. As they disappeared from view, Jennifer let out a hearty laugh. "That boy is going to be so traumatized," she chuckled, earning a playful swat on the arm from Tanya.

David, still calmly eating his chicken salad, simply raised an eyebrow. "Traumatized? Please. He's a Renado. He'll be back in an hour asking for pointers." Summer snorted with laughter, "Pointers? From you, David? On that? I'd pay to see that."

The remaining women erupted into a chorus of laughter, the sound echoing through the fortified dining room. Even the normally stoic Elena cracked a smile. "I just hope he remembers to use protection," Kayla said, earning a chorus of knowing glances. "We don't need any more surprise Renaldo's running around." "Oh, relax," Jessica said, waving her hand dismissively. "They're downstairs. The bunker is stocked with enough Trojans to take over the Greek empire.

Downstairs, in Lily and Josh's room, a space that could only be described as a tactical farm-girl's paradise. Josh sprawled on the bed, a testament to honest labor and youthful enthusiasm. His farmer's tan was a roadmap of sunny days spent tending the ranch, and his usually neatly combed hair was delightfully disheveled. He was, quite simply, trying to catch his breath.

Lily, on the other hand, was practically buzzing with unspent energy. Starkly naked against the backdrop of navy-blue sheets, her pale skin seemed to glow. A single, platinum braid snaked around her neck, framing a face that was pure, unadulterated mischief. While Josh was content to rest, Lily was anything but. "Come on, Josh," she urged, her voice a playful weapon. "Is that all you've got?" Josh groaned, a sound that was equal parts exhaustion and reluctant amusement. "Lily-baby," he managed, his voice still raspy, "I swear, you're like a little... bunny. A very, very dangerous bunny."

Lily giggled, a sound that was both innocent and utterly knowing. She bounced lightly on the edge of the bed, the movement sending a ripple through the blankets that partially covered Josh. "Dangerous bunnies have more fun, don't they?" She leaned closer, her fingers tracing the line of his jaw. "Besides, don't you want to fuck this cute little body of mine again?" Josh rolled his eyes, but a smile tugged at the corner of his lips. "You are incorrigible, you know that, right?" He reached out, gently pulling her closer. "And right now, I need to focus on recovering."

Lily playfully nipped at his ear. "Then you should eat, so you can get your strength up?" Josh chuckled. "I didn't bring anything to…" Lily silenced him with a firm seal on his mouth. Just as she wrapped his nose with her labia, she removed the sheet covering him. "And while you eat, I'm going to suck this little guy," Lily smirked.

A few doors down, in Seo-yeon's room, Brian's initial nervousness melted away with each stolen touch. He had wanted Seo-Yeon for months, every fiber of his being drawn to her quiet strength and unwavering kindness. David, after all, had raised him to be a protector, and Seo-Yeon was someone he desperately wanted to protect, and cherish. He gently cupped her face, his thumbs tracing the delicate curve of her cheekbones. Her dark eyes, usually filled with a quiet reserve, were now alight with a vulnerability that made his heart ache. "Are you sure about this, Seo-Yeon?" he asked, his voice laden with emotion. "I don't want you to feel pressured."

She leaned into his touch, her hands finding his. "I've never been more sure of anything, Brian," she whispered, her voice trembling slightly. "I…I want this. I want you." His heart soared. He leaned in and kissed her, a soft, tentative pressure that gradually deepened into something more. He tasted the sweetness of her lips, the warmth of her breath, and a wave of pure, unadulterated desire washed over him. Brian pulled her closer, deepening the kiss. His hands moved with hesitant reverence, exploring the curves of her back, tracing the line of her spine. He tasted every inch of her skin, kissing every part of her body.

Seo-Yeon helped Brian remove her swimsuit. The fabric slid down her slender frame, pooling at her feet. Brian's breath hitched. He didn't want to rush; every touch, every kiss needed to be savored. He wanted her to know that she was beautiful, desirable, and loved. He kissed her belly, moving lower, licking and tasting her skin. Seo-Yeon moaned and tangled her fingers in his hair. His hands held her hips with reverence.

Seo-Yeon's small body nearly disappeared under Brian's broad shoulders as he entered her. She gasped softly, her fingers digging into his back. He paused, his gaze locked with hers, searching for any sign of discomfort. He found only acceptance, trust, and a burning desire mirroring his own. He began to move, slowly at first, then with increasing urgency. The world narrowed to the feel of her soft skin against his, the sound of her breath in his ear, the taste of her lips as he kissed her deeply. He lost himself in the moment, consumed by a primal need that he had never known existed.

But the most... active scene was unfolding in David's room. The sounds emanating from behind the closed door were unmistakable: the rhythmic thud of skin on skin, a woman's breathless gasps, and a low, guttural groan. Inside, Jessica was tied spread-eagled across David's bed, her face flushed, her long wavy blonde hair a mess. David, his eyes blazing with an intensity that bordered on feral, was delivering her a rough serving of David. "That's it, baby," he growled, his voice thick with lust. "Beg for it." Jessica whimpered, bucking against the restraints. "Please, Daddy... harder..." David obliged, his hand connecting with her ass with a resounding smack. Jessica cried out, a mix of pleasure and pain.

In the main living room, Tiffany, Summer, Elena, Taylor, Nicole, and Kayla were gathered, attempting to maintain some semblance of normalcy. "Anyone heard from Lynn?" Tiffany asked, mock concern etched on her face. Josh's mother, blissfully unaware of the true extent of the situation, lived a hundred miles away and was likely driving herself mad with worry about her son. "I would call, but there's no signal," Summer said, her brow furrowed. "Maybe we should send someone to check on her." Elena snorted. "Knowing Lynn, she's probably already packed her bags and is halfway here, ready to helicopter-parent Josh into oblivion."

The rhythmic thumping from down the hall became more pronounced, accompanied by a particularly loud shriek from Jessica. Nicole winced. "Should we... check on them?" Taylor shook her head. "They're fine. Just... expressing themselves." Kayla raised an eyebrow. "Expressing themselves loudly." Tiffany sighed. "Let's just say David is... relieving stress. And Jessica seems to be enjoying it." The wives exchanged knowing glances.

Just then, the door to the living room burst open and Lily, her hair still slightly disheveled, skipped through. "Anyone want to play Monopoly? I'm feeling competitive." Tiffany, Summer, and Taylor perked up at the idea of a distraction. Nicole, however, remained fixed, a knot of concern twisting in her stomach. Jessica hadn't sounded like she was enjoying herself. Not really. "I'm going to check on her," she announced, her voice firm despite the tremor in her hands.

Elena, lounging on the couch with a book, lowered it just enough to peer over the top. "Nicole, honey, trust me, you don't want to interrupt whatever's happening in there. For your own safety." Elena's warning only amplified Nicole's unease. It wasn't like David to be...rough, unless that was explicitly what Jessica wanted. And that last shriek...it didn't sound consensual. Her sweet, trusting nature rebelled at the thought of Jessica being in distress. "I'm just going to make sure she's okay," Nicole insisted, pushing past Elena and heading down the hall towards David's room.

Meanwhile, Lily was already setting up the Monopoly board on the large coffee table. "Alright, ladies, who wants to lose first?" she declared with a mischievous grin. "I call the top hat!" Tiffany exclaimed, grabbing the silver token before anyone else could. Summer, ever the pragmatist, chose the battleship for its defensive capabilities, while Taylor opted for the Scottie dog, claiming it was "the cutest."

Nicole approached David's door with trepidation. It was slightly ajar, and the sounds emanating from within were even more harrowing than she'd imagined. She could hear David's deep voice, rough and commanding, and Jessica's cries, a mix of pain and...something else she couldn't quite decipher. Taking a deep breath, Nicole pushed the door open further and stepped inside.

Inside, Jessica was indeed tied to the bed, tears running down her face. David's naked physique was both intimidating and arousing. Nicole froze, a deer caught in the headlights.

David and Jessica stopped, both turning to look at Nicole. David's eyes, usually warm and hazel, were now focused with an intensity that made Nicole's knees weak. "Shut the door," he commanded, his voice soft but firm.

Nicole, without a word, pushed the door closed behind her. "I...I was worried about Jessica," she stammered, her voice hesitant. Her heart pounded against her ribs, a frantic drum solo against the unsettling silence that followed. Without breaking eye contact with Nicole, a slow smile spreading across his face, David untied Jessica. The pregnant woman, still teary-eyed, but now sporting a distinctly wicked grin, hopped off the bed. They both descended on Nicole like cultists stumbling upon a virgin sacrifice. Jessica and David walked Nicole to the bed and started removing her clothes, Nicole still too scared to move.

Meanwhile, in the living room, Taylor, Summer, and Tiffany were still engrossed in a surprisingly cutthroat game of Monopoly. Tiffany was ruthlessly buying up Boardwalk and Park Place, while Summer meticulously tracked every transaction. Taylor was trying to negotiate peace, a futile effort in the face of Tiffany's capitalist zeal. Elena, draped elegantly on the couch, remained absorbed in her book, occasionally glancing up with a knowing smirk. Kayla, sprawled on a beanbag chair, was watching "Spaceballs", occasionally laughing and offering deadpan commentary.

Jennifer and Tanya walked into the living room, looking refreshed after their showers. Tanya's long black hair was still damp, clinging to her shoulders, while Jennifer's blonde bob was perfectly styled. "Hey, where's Nicole?"

Tanya asked, noticing the missing member. Elena, without looking up from her book, drawled, "She went to check on Jessica. Apparently, things got a little...vocal." Jennifer snorted, a mischievous glint in her eyes. "Oh, she's gonna get fucked to within an inch of her life. That's what happens when you interrupt Master's playtime with Jessica."

Summer, momentarily distracted from the Monopoly board, raised an eyebrow. "Jennifer, really? Could you be a little more delicate? Nicole can be...sensitive." "Sensitive?" Jennifer scoffed. "She'll be sore, maybe, but she'll be fine. Besides," she added with a wink, "she's been asking for it." Tiffany, ever practical, chimed in. "Alright, ladies, let's not gossip. We have a game to win. Tanya, you're up. Are you buying Mediterranean Avenue or not?"

Several hours later, the Monopoly board on the coffee table was a battlefield. Tiffany, with her signature competitive gleam, clutched Boardwalk and Park Place like they were life rafts. Summer, ever the strategist, meticulously managed her tiny plastic houses, muttering about ROI. Taylor, the kindest of the bunch, was getting systematically bled dry, her brow furrowed in concentration as she desperately tried to avoid landing on Tiffany's empire. And Lily, perched on the edge of the sofa, fueled the chaos with witty commentary, occasionally offering terrible advice to Taylor just to watch the fireworks. "Seriously, Taylor, mortgage everything and buy railroads! Trust me," Lily chirped, her platinum curls bouncing.

David, sipping his hot orange tea in his favorite armchair, chuckled. He watched the domestic squabble unfold with an amusement that bordered on fondness. The apocalypse might be raging outside, but within these walls, the petty dramas of Monopoly lived on. He took another sip of his tea, the citrusy warmth a pleasant contrast to the faintly chaotic energy of the room. He was, as always, unruffled.

Just then, Seo-Yeon stumbled into the living room, her face flushed, her usually impeccable hair a mess. She gripped the doorframe for support, looking like she'd just run a marathon...backwards. "Water," she croaked, her voice barely a whisper. "I need water." Jennifer, perched on the arm of the couch, dissolved into giggles. Elena, leaning against the wall, arched a knowing eyebrow. "Rough gardening session, Seo-Yeon?" Jennifer managed to choke out between giggles.

Seo-Yeon glared, or at least tried to, before collapsing onto the nearest chair, gasping for breath. "Brian," she managed to wheeze, "has the stamina of a... a cyborg!" The room erupted. Even Tiffany, usually laser-focused on bankrupting Taylor, snorted with laughter. Lily, ever quick on the draw, seized the opportunity. "Welcome to the Recovery Ward, Seo-Yeon! We have tea, sympathy, and a healthy dose of schadenfreude."

Meanwhile, across the room, Nicole was a picture of blissful exhaustion. She lay sprawled on the recliner, still in her pajamas, her long silver hair fanned out around her head. Her legs slightly parted, a small, contented sigh escaped her lips. She felt... boneless. "Remind me to never interrupt David and Jessica again," she murmured, mostly to herself. "I think I actually left my body at one point." Elena and Jennifer exchanged a mischievous glance. "Oh, but you looked like

36

you enjoyed yourself, Nicole," Elena purred, earning her a playful swat from Nicole.

Jessica, who was currently cradling Luci, entered the room. "What's all the ruckus?" she asked, her voice a soft murmur. "Just another victim of the Renado Madness," Jennifer said, earning a glare from Jessica. David, still observing the scene with detached amusement, took another sip of his tea. It was a testament to his… dedication, really, that he could still enjoy a cup of tea after all that. "Anyone hungry?" Kayla poked her head in from the kitchen. "I was thinking of making some sandwiches." "Sandwiches sound amazing!" Taylor exclaimed, relieved to have an excuse to escape the Monopoly game.

Jennifer simply shook her head, a motherly smile playing on her lips. Seo-Yeon, mortified but secretly pleased by the attention, blushed even harder. "It was…intense," she stammered, grabbing a glass of water Tanya offered her. "He… he wouldn't stop!" David chuckled, patting Lily's head. "That's my boy. Taking initiative, just like his old man." Jessica snorted. "Initiative? Honey, that sounds like a full-blown hostile takeover!"

The ribbing continued, good-natured and hilarious. Even the dachshunds seemed to sense the lighter mood, wagging their tails tentatively. The Monopoly game was forgotten, replaced by a healthy dose of gossip and teasing.

Chapter 3

The Helicopter Parent

Lynn wrung her hands, the floral print of her pants clashing violently with the grim anxiety plastered across her face. Four days. Four days since the damned internet had vanished, taking with it reruns of "Murder, She Wrote," online coupons, and most importantly, communication with her darling Josh. He hadn't called. She couldn't call him. The silence was deafening, a constant, buzzing reminder of her maternal inadequacy. Every unanswered minute chipped away at her resolve, planting seeds of worst-case scenarios in her overactive imagination. Had he run out of food? Was he hurt? Or, the thought she dared not voice, had something... worse... happened?

Her parents, bless their cotton socks and casserole dishes, were not helping. They treated the blackout as a minor inconvenience, something to be solved with extra ice in the cooler and a stern talking-to from the power company, who, as far as Lynn could tell, had probably vanished into thin air. Her father was currently wrestling a side of beef into their already groaning freezer, muttering about the good old days when meat was preserved with salt and grit. The pungent aroma of raw meat and the rhythmic thud of it being shoved into the already overstuffed freezer were doing little to ease Lynn's mounting anxiety. "Dad, shouldn't we be rationing?"

Lynn squeaked, earning a withering glare from her mother. "Rationing? Lynn, dear, don't be dramatic. We've got enough food here to feed a small army. Besides," she patted Lynn's hand with a chillingly calm smile, "Josh will be fine. He's a farm boy, remember? He knows how to survive." Easy for her to say. She didn't know David.

That man... David. Lynn shuddered. He'd always been polite, disturbingly so, but there was something about him that set her teeth on edge. All that talk of preparedness, the strange fortress of a house he'd built miles outside of town, the almost unsettlingly well-behaved children... It was all too... calculated. He seemed to anticipate problems, which in itself was unsettling. The way he looked at you, like you were a chess piece he was contemplating moving across a board. And that last phone call. She had just wanted to ask about Josh, to hear his voice, but David had been so cold, so dismissive. "Lynn, now is not a good time. The phones will be down soon, so I'm cutting this conversation short. Josh is safe." Click. The nerve! "I'm going," Lynn announced, grabbing her purse. "Going where, dear? The grocery store's closed, and the roads are probably jammed." "I'm going to see Josh." Lynn's voice trembled, but her resolve, fueled by panic and a generous helping of maternal guilt, was firm.

Her mother sighed, a sound like air hissing from a punctured tire, a sound that seemed to drain all the remaining hope from the room. "Lynn, it's a hundred miles! And with no gas..." "I'll walk if I have to!" Lynn declared, picturing herself, a one-woman army of floral print, braving the Texas wilderness to rescue her son. She imagined herself fending off wild dogs, outsmarting desperate scavengers, all fueled by the burning need to see Josh safe. The image was almost heroic, if it weren't so utterly terrifying.

Lynn gripped the steering wheel of her hand-me-down SUV, knuckles white. The abandoned cars were becoming more frequent, forming metal graveyards in the middle of the highway. It had only been a few days, but society was already starting to fray at the edges. Panic was a palpable thing, hanging thick in the air like the smoke from nearby accidents. The radio, long silent, was just another useless piece of metal, a reminder of the world she had lost.

Lynn pressed her lips into a thin line. She had to reach Josh. She had to make sure he was safe. David, that stubborn, infuriating, yet undeniably competent man, was her only hope. Even if he did hang up on her. She clung to the image of Josh's smiling face, the memory of his last hug. Those memories were her fuel, her compass, guiding her through the growing chaos.

Meanwhile, back at the fortress of Renado, David was gearing up. The rhythmic click-clack of metal and plastic snaps was a soothing counterpoint to the chaos he knew was unfolding beyond their valley. He moved with a practiced efficiency, his movements precise and economical. "Daddy, are we going to get Miss Lynn?" Lily asked, skipping into the armory. "Yes, munchkin. We are. But you need to stay close to me, understand?" David replied, checking the magazine. "Things are getting messy out there." Lily nodded seriously, grabbing her P365 and M4 off the wall. David chuckled, ruffling her hair. "You are the best protector. But even protectors need backup."

Tiffany walked in, her blonde braid swinging behind her. She was already dressed in practical cargo pants, a fitted t-shirt and her plate carrier, her Colt Python holstered at her hip. She was the picture of calm competence, a stark contrast to the escalating panic outside. "Ready to roll?" she asked. "Almost," David replied, holstering his Beretta. "Just need to grab a few things. And remind me why I agreed to this again?" "Because Josh is a good man, and he loves your daughter," Tiffany said, her eyes narrowing slightly. "And because Lynn, despite her… quirks, is still his mother."

David sighed. "Fine, fine. But she complains about one thing, one single thing… I'm dropping her off on the side of the road." After grabbing a spare carrier, David reached for his wakizashi, a familiar feeling coursing through his veins. It was more than just a weapon; it was a reminder of his time alone. "Elena!" David called out. As they left David's room, Jessica and Elena came running. "You're in charge until I get back, make sure Kyle and David get relieved in an hour and if anyone comes over, give them crackers and water, but keep them outside," he said as he kissed Jessica.

David steered the modified van through the gridlocked highway, Tiffany beside him, Lily in the back, humming a tuneless melody. The journey was slow and agonizing. Abandoned cars littered the road, forcing David to navigate through the wreckage. He saw signs of desperation: shattered windows, ransacked vehicles, and the occasional figure lurking in the shadows, their eyes hollow with hunger

41

and fear. "People are already losing it," Tiffany observed grimly. "It's only been a few days." David nodded. "That's why we need to get Lynn and go back. The longer we're out here, the more dangerous it becomes.

After what felt like an eternity, they finally arrived at Lynn's parents' house. It was a modest rural house, looking woefully unprepared for the unfolding chaos. Still littered with unfinished projects and empty flower pots. David parked the van in front, its imposing presence a stark contrast to the cluttered yard. "Stay here," David instructed Tiffany and Lily. "I'll go talk to them."

He approached the front door and knocked. After a moment, Lynn's father, his former father in law, opened the door. "Good afternoon, can I help you?" he asked, his tone wary. "I'm here to pick up Lynn," David replied. "Josh, my son in law, is worried about her." "Oh! You must be David. I'm sorry but, Lynn's not here," her father said, his eyes darting nervously. "She left a few hours ago. Said she was going to your place."

David's jaw tightened. "She what?" "Yeah, she was worried about Josh and wanted to see if you guys were okay," her father explained. "I tried to talk her out of it, but if you know Lynn. You know she's always been headstrong." David cursed under his breath. Of all the times for Lynn to be brave, it had to be now. "Did she say what she was driving?" "Her old Black SUV," her father replied. "It's not in the best shape, but it's all she's got."

David thanked him and turned back to the van. "Change of plans," he announced. "Lynn decided to take a solo road trip to our place." Tiffany groaned. "Seriously? That woman has a death wish." "Tell me about it," David muttered. "We need to find her before she gets herself into trouble." They piled back into the van, and David turned the vehicle around. This time, they were heading back the way they came, but with a new sense of urgency. Lynn, most definitely unprepared, was out there somewhere, navigating the increasingly dangerous roads.

As they drove, David tried to think like Lynn. Where would she go? What would she do? He knew she was determined, but also impulsive and prone to making rash decisions. He knew that Lynn's anxiety often manifested as action, even if that action was ill-conceived. "She probably thinks she's being helpful," Tiffany said, reading David's expression. "But she's just making things worse." "I know," David replied. "But as much as I'd like to. We can't leave her out there. She's Josh's mother, and Lily loves Josh."

They continued their search, scanning the road for any sign of the black SUV. The sun began to set, casting long shadows across the highway. The abandoned cars looked even more menacing in the dim light. The orange glow painted the scene in hues of impending doom. Suddenly, Lily shouted from the back. "Daddy, look! Over there!" David followed her gaze and saw a familiar vehicle pulled over to the side of the road. It was a black SUV, and it looked like it had seen better days.

He pulled the van over and jumped out, his heart pounding in his chest. He approached the SUV cautiously, his hand resting on his Beretta. As he got closer, he saw Lynn sitting behind the wheel, looking flustered and scared. The car had a flat tire, and she was clearly struggling to change it. "Lynn! What are you doing out here?" David asked, his voice a mixture of relief and exasperation.

Lynn looked up, her eyes wide with surprise. "David! What are you doing here? I was coming to your place." "I know," David said. "Your dad told me. What happened to your tire?" "I don't know," Lynn replied. "I just heard a pop, and then the car started swerving. I've never changed a tire before." David sighed. Of course, she hadn't.

David's mind, even in the relative calm of their fortified van, was a whirlwind of calculations. Lynn was a variable he hadn't accounted for, a chaotic element introduced into his meticulously planned equation for survival. As they prepared to load Lynn into the back of the armored Ford Transit, a glint of metal caught his eye. It wasn't the dull sheen of a discarded can, nor the reflection off a shattered window. This was something different: a deliberate glare, the kind that spoke of intent, of malice. He tensed, his senses heightened, the world narrowing to a razor's edge. Someone was watching them.

"Stay in the van," he commanded, his voice low and sharp, instantly snapping Tiffany and Lily to attention. He felt the shift in the air, the subtle change in the wind that carried a scent of desperation and malice. It wasn't a conscious thought, just a primal awareness honed by years of hard earned experience. He knew what was coming, even before he saw them.

From behind the hulks of abandoned cars, they emerged – a ragged band of young men, barely old enough to shave, clutching an assortment of firearms. Their eyes were hollow, reflecting the gnawing hunger and fear that David knew all too well. They were desperate, and that made them dangerous, unpredictable. "Get out of the van! Now!" one of them yelled, his voice cracking with a nervous bravado that didn't fool David for a second. "We need that vehicle!"

Lynn gasped, fumbling with the door handle. David didn't have time for this. He didn't have time to negotiate, to reason, or to explain. These men weren't looking for a conversation; they were looking for a score, a means to survive another day, regardless of the cost. Before Tiffany or Lily could react, David was a blur of motion. His Beretta remained holstered. Instead, his hand flashed to his side, drawing the Wakizashi – the shorter, more agile blade that had become his weapon of choice.

The Wakizashi, a gleaming extension of his will, sang through the air. The first attacker, a skinny kid holding a generic shotgun, didn't even have time to scream. The blade found its mark with surgical precision. The next two, emboldened by their numbers, charged forward. David sidestepped, a dance of death, and the smaller sword flashed again, silencing them before they could level their weapons.

A fourth attempted to flank him, but David spun, the Wakizashi a whirlwind of steel. The young man stumbled back, clutching his throat, before collapsing in a gurgling heap. The whole thing was over in seconds, a brutal ballet of violence executed with terrifying efficiency.

David stood panting slightly, the Wakizashi dripping crimson in the fading light. His eyes, usually bright with compassion, were now cold and distant. He flicked the blade, sending a shower of blood onto the cracked asphalt. The highway was silent once more, save for the ragged breaths of those who remained. Lynn stared at him, her face pale, her eyes wide with terror. She had never seen anything like this, this brutal, efficient violence. This wasn't the David she knew. This man was a predator, lethal and unburdened by conscience.

He sheathed the Wakizashi, the click of the blade a stark punctuation mark. He turned to Lynn, his expression softening slightly, but the steel remained in his eyes. "Get in the van, Lynn," he said, his voice devoid of emotion. "Now." He glanced at her SUV, a black tomb sitting on a flat tire. "Forget the car," he said, his voice flat. "It's a lost cause." He knew the scavengers would be here soon, stripping it of everything of value. They would descend like vultures, picking clean the bones of the fallen and the abandoned. Blood, gasoline, desperation – it was a siren song in this new, brutal world. He didn't have time to waste on sentimentality. Survival demanded pragmatism, a hard, unwavering focus on the present. He had a family to protect, a sanctuary to maintain. Every second wasted was a gamble with their lives.

Tiffany, her face pale but resolute, ushered a trembling Lynn into the van. She'd read about this David in his journals, the ruthlessly efficient survivor he had become in the face of unrelenting horror. Long before the world crumbled, David had been preparing, meticulously studying survival techniques, martial arts, and the art of self-reliance. His foresight, once dismissed as eccentricity, was now their lifeline. But seeing it firsthand was… different. Her admiration for his strength, his unwavering commitment to protecting his family, deepened. The man was a force of nature, a shield against the encroaching darkness.

Lily, however, watched her father with a different kind of awe. A flicker of something similar sparked in her own eyes. She'd sensed the danger, the underlying threat. The men he'd killed had radiated malice, a predatory hunger that chilled her to the bone. And she'd seen her father neutralize it. Pride swelled in her chest. There was a primal understanding between them, a shared knowledge of the brutal realities they now faced. She wasn't just his daughter; she was his protégé, learning to navigate this dangerous landscape.

Lynn, huddled in the back of the van, was speechless. The casual brutality, the terrifying speed, the complete lack of remorse… She had never imagined David, kind, eccentric, awkward man she'd known, could be capable of such violence. She stared out the window, the image of the fallen men burned into her mind. The way they had lunged, their faces contorted with rage and greed. The sickening thud of the blade. The finality of their collapse. Fear, raw and primal, gripped her. This was not the David she remembered. This was something… else. Something dangerous. Something she couldn't understand. She wondered if she had made a terrible mistake. Perhaps she was safer facing the dangers of the road alone than entrusting her life to this transformed man.

David gripped the steering wheel, his knuckles white. His gaze remained fixed on the long, abandoned road leading back to his ranch. Each mile was a victory, a step further away from the chaos and closer to safety. Beside him, Tiffany kept a watchful eye on Lynn, who sat rigidly in the back, the armored vest feeling less like protection and more like a shroud. "You're not allowed to complain. You're not allowed to interfere," David stated, his voice flat, devoid of inflection. The words hung in the air, heavy and unambiguous. He wasn't delivering a request; it was an edict. He couldn't afford distractions, couldn't risk dissent. He needed her compliance, her unquestioning obedience. His family's survival depended on it.

Lynn swallowed hard, her throat suddenly dry. She managed a shaky nod, avoiding eye contact. The air in the van felt thick with unspoken tension, a suffocating blend of fear and distrust. She was an outsider, an unknown quantity in their carefully constructed world.

Tiffany placed a reassuring hand on Lynn's trembling knee, offering a small, sympathetic smile. "He just wants to keep everyone safe, Lynn. We all do." It was a gentle attempt to soothe, but Lynn wasn't sure if she believed it. Safe? Was this what safe looked like now? Death in the eyes, a sword in his hand? Lily, sat quietly in the passenger seat with her arms crossed, watched the exchange but said nothing. She understood her father. Safety wasn't a passive state; it was a prize earned through vigilance and, if necessary, decisive action. It was a responsibility they all shared.

The white plantation-style house materialized in the twilight, a beacon of order and security in a landscape scarred by ruin. It should have been a welcoming sight, but to Lynn, after what she had just witnessed. It now carried a whisper of something unknown. Something sinister. As they pulled up to the wrap-around porch, she couldn't help but notice the subtle differences she hadn't registered before. There were no powerlines, no vents on the roof, and she never saw a car in front of the house. It was as if the house was detached from the world, self-contained, a fortress against the encroaching chaos.

As the van circled around the west side of the house, David stopped. The massive garage door began to lift, slowly revealing Brian, standing beside the control box. Brian's face was grim, his eyes scanning the surroundings with practiced vigilance. David slowly pulled into the underground garage as Lynn, now hyper aware, noticed the two foot thick walls surrounding them. "Where are the rest of the cars?" Lynn asked, her eyes scanning the massive garage space. The cavernous space was mostly empty, save for the armored van and a few boxes of tools. David didn't respond, he simply opened the door, letting everyone out of the van before heading upstairs. "The cars are put away," Tiffany answered, as she helped Lynn remove her carrier. "Go ahead and go upstairs, the others are expecting you."

Lynn languidly climbed the concrete steps, following David as he walked into the living room. "Daddy's home!" Jessica screamed, clapping her hands. The remaining women waited, their faces etched with concern. Jennifer, Summer,

Elena, Taylor, Nicole, Kayla and Tanya stood shoulder to shoulder, a united front. They were a kaleidoscope of beauty – blonde bobs, platinum curls, long black hair cascading down their backs – but their expressions were uniformly serious. They'd been anticipating their arrival, awaiting David's report. They were a sisterhood, bound together by shared adversity and a fierce loyalty to David. "Everything alright, Master?" Jennifer asked, her voice laced with concern.

David's gaze swept over his wives. "We're fine. Lynn is with us. She needs... accommodation." That single word, "accommodation," spoke volumes. It wasn't "welcome" or "help." It was "manage." Lynn was now a variable in their carefully calculated equation, a potential disruptor of their hard-won equilibrium. It stirred unease amongst them. They had carefully cultivated their life here. Lynn was an unknown to be managed. Immediately, they went into action. Kayla took Lynn's arm gently but firmly. "Come with me, Lynn. Let's get you a room."

As Lynn was guided back down stairs, followed by Summer and Elena, Jessica approached David, her eyes filled with worry. "Daddy, what happened?" David knelt to her level, his hand cupping her cheek. "There were... complications, Baby. But it's over." He knew this wouldn't be easy. Lynn was a loose end from his past, a ghost he thought he'd buried. Now, she was here, a stark reminder of the life he'd left behind – a naive, trusting life that had no place in this new world.

Inside, Lynn was ushered into a guest room. It was beautifully furnished, comfortable, and surprisingly well-stocked. A stark contrast to the desolate world outside. But even the softest duvet and the most luxurious amenities couldn't dispel the chilling fear that clung to her. Kayla handed her a glass of water. "Drink this, Lynn. You look like you've seen a ghost." Lynn accepted the glass, her hand shaking slightly. "I... I have," she whispered, her gaze fixed on the floor. "I saw David... he..." "He did what he had to do," Elena interjected, her voice firm but not unkind. "This world is different now, Lynn. You either adapt, or you die." Her words were a warning, a veiled threat.

Summer sat beside her on the bed. "We understand this is a lot to take in. But we're here for you. We'll help you adjust." But Lynn wondered if she could adjust. Could she reconcile the image of the monster she'd seen on the highway with her memory of the man she thought she knew? Could she ever truly trust him? Could she ever feel safe within these walls, knowing the price of safety was obedience and acceptance of a world turned upside down? The water tasted like ash in her mouth.

Chapter 4

Misinformation Campaign

The aroma of frying bacon and brewing coffee filled the air, a stark contrast to the chaos raging beyond the valley. Lynn sat at the large kitchen island, her eyes darting around, trying to reconcile this domestic scene with the image of David coolly dispatching those men last night. Josh, surprisingly calm, sat beside her, offering a reassuring smile. Summer moved around the kitchen with the practiced ease of a seasoned chef, expertly flipping pancakes and cracking eggs.

"So," Lynn began, her voice a little shaky. "This… must be quite a place, Josh." Josh chuckled nervously. "Yeah, well, it takes some getting used to." He paused, then added with a strained smile, "Understatement of the century, probably."

Summer, without missing a beat, placed a steaming plate of pancakes in front of Lynn. "Eat up. You need to keep your strength up. It's going to be a long day." Lynn took a tentative bite. The pancakes were delicious, fluffy and sweet. But the taste was overshadowed by the unease churning in her stomach.

"Summer, how… how is everything still working?" Lynn asked, gesturing around the kitchen. "The lights, the stove… everything." Summer smiled knowingly. "David planned for everything, Lynn. Solar power, generators, a backup for the backup. We're completely off-grid." Lynn's jaw dropped. "Off-grid? Since when?"

Before Summer could answer, the kitchen door swung open and Tiffany strode in, her current disposition a stark contrast from the night prior. She was dressed in plaid pajama pants and a t-shirt, still looking every bit the capable woman David would have chosen as his partner. "Morning, everyone," she said cheerfully, grabbing a mug and filling it with coffee. "Lynn, did you sleep okay?"

Lynn hesitated, unsure how to answer. "As well as I could, I guess. It's just... a lot to process." Tiffany nodded understandingly. "I can imagine. But don't worry, we're all here for you. We'll help you make sense of it." It was then that Lynn noticed the other women starting to gather. Jennifer, with her chic blonde bob, sauntered in, playfully slapping David's arm as he entered behind her. He just gave her a look that told her to be respectful.

Elena, dark and elegant, poured herself a cup of coffee, her eyes narrowed in a way that suggested she saw right through Lynn's façade. Taylor, sweet and unassuming, offered Lynn a warm smile. Nicole, with her striking silver hair, moved with a quiet grace as she began setting the table. Kayla, ever the pragmatist, was already organizing the breakfast dishes. Jessica, with her long wavy blonde hair, gave David a quick hug. The biggest shock to Lynn wasn't the women individually, it was the collective.

Lynn's head was spinning. She knew these women, or at least, she had known them. They were all friends of Josh, employees, or people she'd met at various gatherings over the

53

years. But she'd never seen them like this, moving in sync, their expressions a mixture of strength and quiet determination. And the way they looked at David, with a mixture of respect, affection, and something else she couldn't quite place. "So," Lynn finally blurted out, unable to contain her curiosity any longer. "Are you all like, his friends?" Tiffany choked on her coffee, stifling a laugh. Jennifer burst out grinning. Elena raised an eyebrow, a hint of amusement playing on her lips.

David calmly stepped forward, placing a hand on Lynn's shoulder. "Lynn, these are my wives." The room went silent. Lynn stared at David, her mouth hanging open, then back at the women, her expression a mixture of shock and disbelief. "Wives? All of you? But... how?" David sighed, running a hand over his head. "It's a long story, Lynn. A very, very long story. But the short version is, we're a family. And right now, we're focused on surviving."

The Initial shock began to wear off, replaced by a growing sense of bewilderment. Lynn had always known David was a bit... different. He was intelligent, resourceful, and had a quiet intensity that she found both intriguing and intimidating. But this? She wasn't emotionally prepared for this.

As the rest of the family began to filter into the kitchen — Aidan and Alissa, Brian and Seo-Yeon, Lily, with her platinum blonde hair mirroring Summer's, David's other children, Seth and Grace, the twins whose unnerving gazes made Lynn slightly uncomfortable — Lynn watched them, trying to piece together the puzzle. They all moved with the same sense of purpose, the same quiet confidence. They laughed, they joked, they bickered, but there was an underlying sense of unity that was undeniable.

Lily, skipping over to David, wrapped her arms around him. "Daddy, can we go practice shooting today?" David smiled down at her. "Maybe later, Sweetheart. We have… guests to entertain." Lynn frowned. The way they talked about "guests" was strange.

As everyone settled down to eat, Lynn couldn't help but notice how seamlessly they all worked together. Aidan and Brian cleared the table, Alissa and Seo-Yeon washed the dishes, Lily helped Summer prepare a second batch of pancakes. The whole process was so efficient, so well-orchestrated, it was almost… robotic.

"Okay, everyone," David announced, clapping his hands together. "Today, we need to focus on preservation. It's going to get hot outside, and we need to be prepared. Josh, you're with me. Aidan, Brian, after you finish your checks, help Kyle with training. The rest of you, continue with your usual routines."

With a flurry of activity, the family dispersed, each heading off to their assigned tasks. Lynn watched them go, her mind reeling. She had come to David's house to find her son, even seeking some kind of refuge. But she had stumbled into something far more complex, far more… intentional. She suddenly realized she was the only one who didn't know what to do.

Summer, ever the picture of serene efficiency, turned to Lynn, a gentle smile gracing her lips. "Come on, Lynn, let's get you settled in." Lynn, still reeling from the whirlwind of the morning, followed Summer, her eyes darting around the bustling kitchen. The rhythmic clanging of pots and pans, the murmur of conversations, the scent of freshly brewed coffee – it was all so…normal, considering the world outside was supposedly collapsing.

They stepped out of the main house and into the crisp morning air. Lynn squinted, taking in the vastness of the property. "Where are we going?" she asked, more out of bewildered curiosity than suspicion. "We're going to get you set up with an apartment," Summer replied, her voice calm and reassuring. "It's not much, but it's comfortable, and it's safe."

Lynn followed Summer as they walked east, past the barn and towards a building that looked suspiciously like a work shed. "An apartment? In… there?" Lynn gestured incredulously at the squat, reinforced-steel structure. She knew about the barn. Josh even worked there through the summers. But this shed? It looked more like a place to store tools than a living space. Summer simply smiled knowingly. "Just trust me, Lynn. And trust David."

They entered the shed, the smell of gun oil and burnt metal filling Lynn's nostrils. Kyle, a young man with an unusually chipper disposition, was scoring plate steel for some new project. He nodded politely at Summer and gave Lynn a curious glance. "Good morning miss Summer." "Morning, Kyle," Summer replied. "Just showing Lynn to her new place." Kyle threw his head up in acknowledgement, before turning his music back up and returning to work.

Summer led Lynn to a set of unassuming concrete stairs tucked in the corner of the shed. "Down we go." Lynn hesitated, a knot of unease tightening in her stomach. "Down? Where does this go?" "You'll see," Summer said, her smile unmoving. "Just a few steps." With a deep breath, Lynn followed Summer down the stairs. The air grew cooler, the sounds of the shed fading above them. As they reached the bottom, Lynn's eyes widened in surprise.

They were in a stark, utilitarian concrete bunker, the air humming with the low thrum of machinery. A row of eight massive generators lined one wall, their presence both intimidating and oddly comforting. "This is…a generator room," Lynn said, stating the obvious. "Indeed," Summer said, her smile widening. "But it's also the lobby. Follow me."

Summer walked past the generators to a heavy steel door. She punched in a code on a keypad, and with a loud clunk, the door swung open, revealing… another set of stairs. But these led to a brightly lit corridor. Lynn stepped through, her jaw dropping.

Before her stretched a long hallway lined with four identical doors on each side. Each door had a small plaque beside it. Probably for displaying a family name. "What…what are these?" Lynn asked, pointing to the pallets of boxes, tucked between each doorway. Summer smiled. "Those are emergency rations. Should last a person up to eighteen years if they're modest, or a small family for about five years. Each apartment gets two pallets."

Before Lynn could examine the rations, Summer grabbed her hand, leading her down the hall. "Welcome to the Apartment bunker," Summer announced, gesturing grandly. "We don't have a fancy name for it yet, but if you have any ideas, drop it in the suggestion box." Lynn just stared, her mind struggling to process what she was seeing. That wasn't just a shed; it was a cleverly disguised entrance to an underground complex. An underground complex filled with apartments. It was insane. And yet, perfectly in line with the David she was getting to know. "Which apartment will I be in?" Lynn asked. "Apartment number 16, at the end of the hall, on ground level… downstairs, sorry, force of habit," Summer said, giggling. "It's all yours. It's fully stocked with everything you'll need."

They walked down the hall to the last apartment, then Summer opened the door. Lynn stepped inside, and found it surprisingly pleasant. Three bedrooms, a small kitchenette, a common room with comfortable seating, and a small but functional bathroom. The furniture was simple but sturdy, and the walls were painted a calming shade of blue. The most surprising feature, however, was the "window." A large LCD screen on the wall displayed a tranquil scene of a forest stream, complete with the sounds of birds chirping and water flowing. It was remarkably convincing.

Lynn touched the screen. "This is…" "A little bit of normalcy," Summer finished. "David thought it would help people adjust. He always thinks of everything. You can also see live feeds of the ranch if you'd prefer." Lynn pushed the buttons on the remote until she saw a view of the front of the house and barn. There, as if her window opened right into the pasture was David and Josh, circling the house as David gestured toward the hilltops.

Lynn walked into the kitchenette and opened one of the cabinets. Canned goods, dried pasta, bottled water — enough to last for weeks. She opened the refrigerator, finding it stocked with fresh produce, dairy products, and even a few bottles of wine. "He has literally thought of everything," Lynn chuckled. "He does," Summer said, her voice filled with affection. "Now, make yourself at home. I'll leave you to settle in. If you need anything, just ask. We're all here to help." Summer turned to leave, but Lynn stopped her. "Summer, wait. Thank you. For…all of this, for everything."

Summer smiled warmly. "You're welcome, Lynn. We're glad to have you." As Summer left, Lynn closed the door and leaned against it, letting out a long, shaky breath. She was safe. She had a roof over her head, food in her belly, and a community of…interesting…people to support her. It was all so surreal, so unexpected. She had come to David's house expecting to rescue her son, but she had stumbled into a prepper's paradise, complete with underground bunkers, miniature cows, and a leader who seemed to have a plan for everything.

Lynn was still taking in the sheer surreality of her apartment bunker when a chorus of chirps, beeps, and ringtones suddenly erupted. She jumped, startled, and looked around wildly. Her phone, once a glorified mp3 player, was buzzing with notifications. "What in the…?" she muttered, cautiously looking at her phone. The screen was flooded with alerts: emails, news headlines, social media updates, all screaming for attention. It was information overload, a sensory assault after days of silent isolation.

Upstairs in the main house, a similar cacophony was unfolding. Cheers and shouts of excitement echoed through the halls. Tiffany, who had been overseeing dinner preparations, dropped a spoon with a clang. "The internet's back!" she exclaimed, wiping her hands on her apron and rushing toward the living room, where the main computer was located. Jessica, nestled on the couch with Homer, let out a groan of disappointment. "Ugh, but TikTok isn't working!" she whined, scrolling through the apps on her phone with a frustrated pout. "What's the point of the apocalypse if I can't criticize stupid people?"

David, who had been reviewing patrol routes with Josh on the back deck, strode into the house, his face a mask of calm amidst the chaos. He surveyed the scene – the jubilant wives, the excited children, the buzzing devices – with a hint of weariness. "Alright, everyone, settle down," he said, his voice cutting through the noise. "Just because the network is back online doesn't mean anything is fixed. It could be temporary, it could be compromised. We need to be cautious."

Lynn, still overwhelmed by the returned connectivity, felt a sense of relief wash over her. Maybe, just maybe, things were going back to normal. Maybe this whole apocalypse thing was just a blip, a temporary glitch in the system. David knew better. He remembered how the infrastructure was fixed, how the network put everyone in a false sense of security. He had seen this before, the false dawn, the fleeting return to normalcy before the final descent into chaos. He knew the network's resurrection wouldn't last. He also knew uninformed people used this opportunity to share information, to brag, even reveal their hidden stockpiles and secrets. Meanwhile, others used this opportunity to gather information, track survivors, and consolidate their power.

He pointed. "Kayla, Brian, Jennifer, Elena, I need you to search the internet. Look for any mention of our family, this house, our stockpile, our ranch. Anything that could compromise our security." Kayla, ever the egalitarian, raised an eyebrow. "Shouldn't we be looking for news about what's happening in the world? Finding out if there's any government response, any relief efforts?" "I already know what's happening, but you do bring up a good point." David pointed again. "Jessica, Taylor, Tanya, Tiffany, find out what's happening, everywhere. I want government actions, locations of extreme civil unrest, anywhere there are safe zones, all of it."

Jennifer was already at the computer, her fingers flying across the keyboard. "Consider it done, Master," she said, her eyes glued to the screen. Brian, ever the tech whiz, set up a series of filters and search parameters. "I'm scrubbing the web for any mentions of prepper communities in central Texas," he said, his brow furrowed in concentration.

As his wives and children diligently scoured the internet, David turned his attention back to Lynn, who was standing hesitantly near the doorway, her eyes wide with a mixture of hope and apprehension. "Lynn," he said, his voice softening. "I know this looks like things are looking up, but it's going to get much worse." Gesturing to the entire room, he ordered. "Don't post anything, and don't tell anyone where you are."

Lynn nodded slowly, her earlier relief fading into a renewed sense of unease. She had seen the ruthlessness in David's eyes when he had defended her the previous night. She knew he wasn't exaggerating. "What can I do?" she asked, her voice barely a whisper. "How can I help?" David smiled, a crooked, almost unnatural smirk. "Just… be Josh's mother. Be a friend to those who need it. And don't start any drama. That's all I ask." She turned and walked back to her apartment.

Back in the apartment bunker, Lynn tentatively reached for her phone. She clicked on a news headline about widespread looting and violence in major cities, and a shiver ran down her spine. She knew David was right. This wasn't over. This was just the beginning. Upstairs, Jennifer suddenly gasped. "Master, I think I found something," she called out, her voice laced with alarm. "Someone's posted a map of prepper locations in Texas. And…and our house is marked." The brief respite of internet connectivity had just turned into a clear and present danger. David's premonition had been right on the mark, and the game had just changed.

The air in the house crackled with a sudden tension. David's face, usually an impassive mask, tightened with barely perceptible fury. "Show me," he commanded, striding over to Jennifer. The image on the tablet was a crude, hand-drawn map of central Texas. Scribbled notes pointed to various locations – rumored bunkers, caches of supplies, and fortified homesteads. A shaky red circle enclosed their valley, with the words "Possible Paramilitary Compound – David's Ranch" scrawled beside it. "Where did you find this?" David asked, his voice dangerously low, his eyes scanning the screen, absorbing every detail. "It was posted on some anonymous forum," Jennifer replied, her fingers flying across the screen. "It's been shared a couple of times, but the original post seems to have been deleted. There's no way to track who uploaded it."

David cursed under his breath. "Damn it. Time to assess the damage." He turned to Aidan and Brian, his sons. "Brian, I want you to run a deep dive on the forum's servers. See if you can pull up any cached versions of the post, IP addresses, anything that can give us a lead." "Right away, Dad," Brian said, already heading towards the office. "Aidan, I need you to monitor all local radio frequencies, all civilian bands. See if you can pick up any chatter about the map, about us. If anyone's planning a visit, we need to know." Aidan, a master of reconnaissance, nodded sharply. "Understood."

Turning to Summer, David said, "Summer, how many people actually saw this posting?" Summer tapped furiously on her keyboard, her brow furrowed. "It's hard to say. The post itself was only up for about twenty minutes before it was taken down, but it was shared on two other forums before that. I'm estimating...maybe a few hundred people at most." "A few hundred too many," David muttered. He knew from the old world that even a handful of determined individuals could cause serious problems. "Elena, I need you to draft a counter-narrative, something to discredit the map. Make us sound like a bunch of harmless survivalists, nothing worth bothering with. Use every tool at your disposal – humor, ridicule, outright lies if necessary."

Elena, a master of propaganda and social manipulation, grinned. "Consider it done, David." He paused, his gaze sweeping over his family. "Tiffany, I want you and Kayla to run a full inventory of our weapons and supplies. Make sure everything is accounted for, and that we're ready for any eventuality." "Already on it," Tiffany replied. "Taylor, Nicole, keep an eye on the perimeter. Double the patrols. I want eyes on every approach, every blind spot." "Yes, David," Taylor said, her voice calm and steady. "Of course, David" Nicole spoke softly.

David turned to Jessica, who was standing near him. "Daddy, what can I do?" she asked, her voice brimming with determination, eager to contribute. David smiled softly, the gruffness melting away. "You stay close, Baby. Keep an eye on Seth and Grace. Make sure they don't get… too curious." Seth and Grace, the twins, were unnervingly observant, their intelligence bordering on unsettling. They were more like information sponges than actual children.

As his wives and children sprang into action, David felt a surge of grim satisfaction. They were a well-oiled machine, each member knowing their role, their responsibilities. He had prepared them for this, trained them for this. He wouldn't let a few anonymous forum posts jeopardize everything he had built. He walked over to the window, his gaze sweeping across the peaceful valley. The sun was shining, the birds were singing, but David knew that beneath the tranquil facade, danger was lurking. They were targets now. And he'd be damned if he'd let anyone take what was his.

He pulled out his phone, which still had limited service. He dialed Kyle's number. "Kyle," he said, his voice curt and businesslike. "I need you to bring every piece of heavy ordinance to the main house, and set them up on the back deck. We've got company coming, whether they know it yet or not." He hung up, the click of the phone echoing in the sudden silence of the room.

David stood in the heart of his command center, the house's expansive kitchen, a mug of lukewarm coffee warming his hands. "Okay, team," David began, his voice calm and measured, a stark contrast to the chaotic data streams scrolling across Brian's custom-built monitors. "The game has changed. They know we're here. Now, we need to decide how they think of us."

Jennifer piped up. "Master, what about just taking them out? Shutting them down?" David shook his head. "Not yet, Jen. We try to manage perception first, then we manage the problem. We need information. Kayla, how's the information network looking?" Kayla, her dark hair pulled back in a practical ponytail, frowned. "We're starting to pick up chatter, David. Mostly confused families, worried about supplies and safety. But I'm seeing an uptick in mentions of our location, too. Mostly whispers. 'The Ranch,' 'The Fortress,' 'The Prepper Compound.'" "Excellent," David said. "Summer, my dear, time to unleash the chaos."

Summer grinned. "Oh, I've been waiting for this! Let's give them a buffet of bullshit. Hippies growing alfalfa, right next to heavily armed revolutionaries with nuclear warheads. How about a cult worshipping miniature cows?" Lily, sprawled on the rug playing with Rahab, and Judas, giggled. "Can we really worship the cows, Daddy? They're so fluffy!" "We can pretend to worship the cows, sweetheart," David corrected, a small smile gracing his lips as he ruffled her hair.

Lynn, huddled awkwardly in a corner, watched the interaction with a mixture of bewilderment and suspicion. This wasn't the hardened, hyper-efficient killer she'd witnessed the night before. This was... Dad? "Seriously, David?" Tiffany asked, raising an eyebrow. "Nuclear warheads? You think people will believe that?" "The point, love, isn't that they believe one thing," David explained, his gaze sweeping over his wives. "The point is that they believe nothing. We flood the zone with so much contradictory nonsense that they can't possibly form a coherent picture of who we are or what we're doing."

Elena chimed in, a malicious twinkle in her eyes. "We can also play on their fears. Rumors of a highly contagious, man-made virus originating from the ranch? Or maybe we're hoarding all the water in the valley?" "Perfect," David said, clapping his hands together. "Taylor, Nicole, limit your patrols to the CCTV monitors, I don't want them to see us coming." "And Lynn," David said, turning his attention to Josh's mother, "please feel free to make yourself useful. You can help Kayla organize the medical supplies, or maybe assist Summer with the... misinformation campaign." David then

66

raised his hand, garnering everyone's attention. "Let's try to use the service tunnels to get back and forth. I know they weren't designed for that purpose, but we still have an underground network."

Lynn, still feeling like an intruder in this bizarre domestic fortress, swallowed nervously. Misinformation? Nuclear warheads? This was far beyond anything she could have imagined. She just wanted to go home.

Chapter 5

The Outsiders Blog

"Okay," David announced, his voice cutting through the domestic hum. "We figured out part of the problem. A local has been gossiping. Which is why our little haven has been labeled a 'possible paramilitary compound' online." Tiffany sighed. "Figures. Small town, big imaginations."

As the misinformation campaign continued, Kyle wandered in. "Hey, David, got a question about night vision. The stuff I have is…adequate, but not exactly cutting-edge." David smiled. "Come with me, Kyle." He led him to the armory, a room that would make any military enthusiast drool. Racks of rifles, pistols, and shotguns lined the walls. Ammunition boxes were stacked neatly. But it was the locked cabinet that David was interested in. He opened it to reveal a treasure trove of military-grade white phosphor night vision optics, 5th generation models, along with a variety of thermal imaging scopes. "Knock yourself out," David said, gesturing expansively. "Take what you need." Kyle's jaw dropped. "Where did you even get all this?" David just shrugged, a hint of a smile playing on his lips. "Let's just say I've been preparing for a rainy day. Or a long, dark night."

Later that afternoon, a cloud of dust announced the arrival of visitors at the ranch. A modified pickup truck rumbled down the long driveway, stopping a respectable distance from the house. Three men and a woman emerged, squinting in the bright Texas sun. They looked determined, prepared, but uncertain. David, flanked by his wives and children, strode out to greet them. He exaggerated his natural awkwardness, stammering slightly as he introduced himself.

"Welcome… uh… welcome to our… uh… ranch," he said, his eyes darting nervously. He gestured to Tiffany, Summer, Jennifer, and Nicole. "These are my… my sisters." Jennifer, decidedly wearing an oversized dress and rubber boots, reached her hand under her skirt. "Bubba, I wanna fuck already," she said, an impatient snarl on her face. Jessica, who had been pulling at him since he left the house, put her hand in his pocket. "Daddy, I can feel your dick." David, feigning frustration, pulled her hand out of his pocket and raised his arm. "I told you, stop call'in me that in front of guests."

His sons, Aidan, Brian, and Little David, were a sight to behold. Aidan, Alissa close by, and Brian carried rusted, broken rifles, their faces smeared with dirt and grease. Little David, not to be outdone, proudly wielded a rusty pipe wrench. They bragged loudly about their "paramilitary training," their voices cracking with adolescent bravado. "We're experts in… uh… tactical maneuvers!" Aidan declared, stumbling slightly as he tried to strike a heroic pose. "And…uh… arm-bushes!" Brian added, nearly dropping his rifle.

Kayla, who approached from the house carrying a tray of drinks, smiled at the guests. "Care for some refreshment?" she offered with a sweet smile. The drinks, however, were a suspect shade of green and smelled like something under the sink. "I'm try'in a new recipe now."

Before anyone could take a sip, Lynn burst out of the house, her voice shrill and piercing. "Kayla! What did I tell you about letting these people drink that poison? And you boys! Put down those dangerous toys before someone gets hurt!" She glared at the visitors, her arms crossed tightly across her chest. "Honestly, this is what happens when you let a bunch of... of... imbeciles run a ranch! I swear, I'm the only one with any lick of sense around here."

She began fussing over Aidan, Brian, and little David, snatching the "weapons" from their hands and scolding them like naughty children. The visitors exchanged bewildered glances. Lynn, now turning to Tiffany, began screaming, "I saw the test in the trash. Are you fucking pregnant again?" Tiffany, while suppressing a giggle, hung her head. "No sissy, bubba said I couldn't get pregnant if I sucked it out before he put it in." Jessica, however, threw gasoline on the fire. "Daddy, we're gonna have a baby!" she shrieked, rubbing her still flat belly.

The visitors shifted uncomfortably. The woman cleared her throat. "Well, thank you for the... uh... hospitality," she said hesitantly. "We should probably be going." They retreated to their truck, climbed inside, and sped away, leaving behind a cloud of dust and a lingering sense of utter confusion.

David watched them go, the corners of his eyes crinkling with amusement. The performance, as bizarre and unsettling as it had been, was a resounding success. He

70

clapped his hands together, the sound sharp in the crisp February air. "Alright, everyone! Back to normal!" he announced, his voice laced with genuine cheer. The shift was immediate. The slouching postures straightened, the vacant stares sharpened with intelligence, and the rusty weapons vanished as if by magic. The air of comical ineptitude dissipated, replaced by an aura of quiet competence.

"You think they bought it?" Summer asked, running a hand through her hair. David nodded. "Hook, line, and sinker. They came expecting a paramilitary stronghold. They left thinking they stumbled into a… well, a very strange, very large, and very dysfunctional family. Exactly what we wanted."

Tiffany smirked. "Kayla's 'refreshments' were a stroke of genius. What was in those, anyway?" Kayla shrugged, her dark eyes twinkling. "A little bit of everything, actually. Plus a bit of old diesel and antifreeze." David chuckled. "And the effect was magnificent. Thank you all. You played your parts perfectly." He turned to Brian, who was already tapping away on a tablet. "Brian, how goes the digital reconnaissance?"

Brian looked up, his brow furrowed in concentration. "I'm tracking the online chatter, Dad. It's proving difficult. The initial source seems to be using multiple VPNs and encrypted channels. But I'm getting closer. I have a few leads, individuals who mentioned the ranch, vaguely, before the blackout." "Vaguely isn't enough, son," David said, his tone firm but gentle. "We need to know who started this, and why. The internet is back online, and the world is watching.

Narrow it down to people that have actually been here. I have lists in my room."

Just then, Jessica stepped forward, her cheeks flushed, a hesitant smile playing on her lips. She was still petite, still sassy, still his Jessica. But there was something different about her today, a soft glow that radiated from within. "Daddy?" she said, her voice a shaky whisper. All eyes turned to her, the playful banter silenced. David knelt, taking her hands in his. "What is it, Baby?" She took a deep breath. "I... I really am pregnant."

The silence that followed was broken only by the chirping of birds in the nearby trees. David stared at Jessica, his expression unreadable. Then, slowly, a wide, genuine smile spread across his face, chasing away the lines of worry that had etched themselves there over the past week. "Pregnant?" he repeated, his voice thick with emotion. "Really?" Jessica nodded, tears welling up in her eyes. "Really, Daddy." David pulled her into a tight embrace, burying his face in her wavy blonde hair. "That's... that's wonderful, Jessica. Absolutely wonderful."

The other wives surged forward, showering Jessica with congratulations. Tiffany wrapped her arms around both David and Jessica. Summer offered a soft smile. Elena clapped Jessica on the back, a mischievous glint in her eyes. Taylor squeezed Jessica's hand, her kind eyes filled with joy. Nicole simply beamed. Kayla, was already worried about baby formula. And Tanya, was already devising a plan to minimize stretch marks. Even Lynn, standing awkwardly on the periphery, seemed genuinely happy for Jessica.

After they finished dinner, Homer, Rahab, and Judas, the lowrider security detail, were strategically positioned, ears perked, noses twitching, ever vigilant against the threat of rogue dust bunnies. The recent blackout, now officially over, according to the flickering remnants of the internet, had left a residue of unease in the air, thicker than Lynn's perfume, which was saying something. "So, ten thousand, give or take a few panicked geriatrics, then?" Jessica asked, cradling her barely-there baby bump. "That's... a lot of people."

David leaned back in his armchair, stroking Luci's dark fur as she sat beside him, looking like a mob villain. Spring is coming early, but the summers will be hotter. "It's a start," he said, his voice calm, even comforting. His wives knew better than to expect emotion. "The weak, the unprepared... they always fall first. It's a thinning of the herd, brutal, but necessary. Nature will be unyielding soon."

Tiffany nodded. "The hospitals were hit hard. Power outages, oxygen failures... it was a bloodbath. Thank God for our generator system." Jennifer, lounging on a nearby sofa, stretched languidly. "Master is always prepared," she purred, earning a playful eye roll from Summer. She loved Jennifer's playfulness. "Daddy's right," Lily piped up. "We're ready for anything."

David fought back a smile. Lily was the embodiment of his hard work. Trained, educated, and utterly adorable. His children were all like that, miniature super soldiers disguised as well-adjusted youngsters. He was absurdly proud of them. Lynn, Josh's mother, puffed up like a disturbed pigeon. "Ready for anything? Josh barely knows how to milk a cow!

And you let him marry a child!" "He's learning," David said flatly, his gaze unwavering. "And Lily is more capable than most adults. Besides, Josh is proficient enough at taking care of the farm animals, and is adapting well.

As for you Lynn, I heard you flushed the toilet twelve times today, you know we have limited water right?" "I'm allowed to flush the toilet!" Lynn retorted, her voice rising. "It's not like we're running out! Not with your fancy bunkers and all." Elena leaned forward. "Oh, Lynn, darling, don't you worry your pretty little head. We have enough water to drown a small continent. But David doesn't like wastefulness, does he?"

Kayla sighed. "Let's not squabble. The important thing is that we use our resources wisely. Has anyone checked the hydroponics lately? Do we need to adjust the nutrient levels?" Jennifer waved her hand dismissively. "The green houses are doing fine, we're actually producing more food than we eat." Suddenly, Brian, perched on the arm of the sofa with Seo-Yeon, spoke up. "The forums are saying the weather patterns are going nuts. Record highs, unseasonal storms... Someone posted a heat advisory in Minnesota, and it's still February."

David mumbled before responding. "That's consistent with what I remember," he said, his voice flat. "The jet stream is destabilizing. We're going to see extreme weather events, droughts, floods... famine." Taylor reached out and squeezed his hand. "This is what you saved us from," she said before kissing him. Nicole nodded in agreement. "And we know you'll get us through this."

Aidan, Alissa beside him, spoke up. "I've been thinking, we should probably figure out how to get clothes for Lynn. I mean, she's not built like mom, or Nicole, or any of them for that matter." David looked at Aidan, a curious smile creeping onto his face. Perhaps he could take her shopping and find a way to leave her there. "What do you think Lynn? Feel like going shopping?" he asked. Lynn just stared back, wide eyed.

Grace, who was petting Rahab's tail chimed in. "We're going to start processing dairy soon. I'm thinking cheese and yogurt, but we'll need more equipment if we're going to want a variety." David raised his eyebrows. "It sounds like we're going to have a busy year. Check the storage for rennet, we may need to start producing some."

David looked over at Brian. "Have you figured out who's been talking shit yet?" Brian sighed. "Almost, but someone made a recent post about us a few minutes ago." David leaned forward. What does it say?" The entire room leaned in, listening intently as Brian read the blog post...

"I recently found myself in a situation so bizarre, so utterly surreal, that I'm still trying to process it. I'd been invited to visit a "ranch," a term I use loosely, given what I encountered. From the moment we arrived, a palpable sense of unease hung in the air, thick enough to cut with a rusty butter knife.

Our host, visibly nervous, introduced his "sisters." One, wearing an oversized dress, immediately demanded intimacy. The others, dirty and smelling of dirt and manure.

Another, a child, reached into his pocket and referred to him in a way that raised immediate red flags. This was... different.

Adding to the unsettling atmosphere were several young men brandishing rusted rifles and a child with a pipe wrench, boasting about their "paramilitary training." Their bravado was undermined by their obvious inexperience, creating a spectacle that was more comical than threatening. They were experts in arm-bushes? I wasn't entirely sure what that was.

Just when I thought things couldn't get any stranger, a lady appeared, offering drinks of a suspicious green hue that smelled vaguely of industrial solvents. Before anyone could partake, an older woman, burst onto the scene, berating the young woman for the "poison" and scolding the "soldiers" like unruly children.

The older woman, clearly the matriarch (or at least the most assertive individual), seemed to be the only one remotely aware of the... unconventional nature of the ranch. Her exasperated pronouncements painted a picture of a family perpetually on the brink of chaos.

As if everything wasn't weird enough. Apparently, that lady saw the results of a home pregnancy test in the trash and began screaming at one of the women if she was pregnant. But she said that she couldn't get pregnant as long as she sucked Bubba first. That's when the little girl shrieked, calling him daddy, and rubbed her flat belly, saying that they were going to have a baby.

The entire visit was a masterclass in awkwardness, leaving me with more questions than answers. What exactly was going on at this "ranch," and how did they manage to function on a daily basis? It was an experience I won't soon forget, though I'm still trying to figure out if I should laugh, cry, or call the authorities."

The room erupted in laughter. Even David couldn't hide his amusement. Wiping his tears, David stood up. "Alright, everyone," he said, his voice regaining authority. "Time for a debriefing. Tiffany, you're in charge of rationing. Jennifer, I need a report on the nutrient levels. David, continue the hand to hand combat training, and help Josh out with that. Summer, I need a complete inventory of our medical supplies, including the antivenom for Lynn."

Lynn spluttered, but David ignored her. "Elena, I want you to monitor the news feeds, find out what's really happening out there. Taylor and Nicole, shadow Tanya and Seo-Yeon for a while, I want you to become experts in comfort, that way we can start cross training Tanya and Seo-Yeon. He turned to Jessica, his youngest wife, and gently brushed a strand of hair from her face. "Baby, Daddy wants you to rest. You and the baby need to stay strong." Jessica beamed, her eyes sparkling with affection. "Yes, Daddy."

As everyone scurried off to bed, David watched his family disperse, each heading to their designated roles within the small, self-sufficient world they were building, or escaping to their beds. He glanced at the clock in the living room. It was nearing ten, time for routine. He followed Jessica back to their room, Lucipurr weaving between their legs, a sleek black shadow.

Jessica, already in her pajamas, was curled up on the bed, petting Lucipurr. The cat purred contentedly, a sound that momentarily eased the tension in the room. Jessica looked up at David, her blue eyes filled with a mix of weariness and happiness. "Daddy," she murmured, holding out her hand.

David sat beside her, taking her hand in his. Her skin was soft, delicate, a stark contrast to his calloused hands. He gently stroked her knuckles, his mind racing through the tasks ahead. "How are you feeling, sweetheart?" he asked, his voice softening. "Tired, but good," she replied, a faint blush rising on her cheeks. "I'm excited about the baby." David placed his hand on her stomach, a wave of tenderness washing over him. "That's my little soldier," he whispered, earning a giggle from Jessica.

Lucipurr hopped onto David's lap, kneading his paws into his thigh. He stroked the cat's fur absently, his thoughts drifting to Tanya. She had been sharing a room with Elena since the blackout, and he wondered if she was ready to return to her own apartment. He valued Tanya's skills and her calm demeanor, and he wanted to ensure she was comfortable. "Jess, I need to check on Tanya," he said, rising from the bed. "I'll be back soon. Get some rest." He leaned down and kissed her forehead, careful not to disturb Lucipurr. As he left the room, he could hear Jessica humming softly, a lullaby for the little one growing inside her.

David found Tanya in the kitchen, brewing a cup of chamomile tea. Elena was at the counter, meticulously cleaning her nails. The two women presented a study in contrasts: Tanya, with her long black hair pulled back in a braid and Elena, with her glamorous air and penchant for provocation. "Tanya, can I have a word?" David asked, his voice polite but firm. Elena raised an eyebrow, a hint of amusement in her eyes. "Going to whisk her away, are you, Master?" she teased.

David ignored her, focusing his attention on Tanya. "I wanted to ask how you're doing, sharing a room with Elena. I know it's not ideal." Tanya sighed, stirring her tea thoughtfully. "It's fine, David. Elena's company is... interesting. But it's not the most restful arrangement." "I understand," David said. "I wanted to know if you'd prefer to move back to your apartment in the morning. I can have Aidan and Brian help you move your things." Tanya hesitated, her gaze flickering towards Elena. "I... I don't know, David. It's been nice having someone to talk to. Elena keeps things lively, even in this... situation."

Elena smirked, blowing on her perfectly manicured nails. "I'm simply a delight to be around, darling. Though I suspect Tanya misses her own space, and your..." she paused, a sultry look in her eyes, "your attentions, David." David felt a flicker of annoyance. Elena enjoyed pushing his buttons, testing his control. He refused to rise to the bait. "Tanya, the choice is yours," he said, his voice steady. "I want you to be comfortable. If you want to stay, that's perfectly acceptable. But if you'd prefer to move back to your apartment, I'll make it happen."

Tanya looked at him, her expression unreadable. He knew she was weighing her options, considering the pros and cons. He also knew that she valued his approval, his understanding. "I'll think about it, David," she finally said, taking a sip of her tea. "Thank you for asking." David leaned in and kissed her sweetly.

His kiss was sweet, a gentle reassurance. It was a kiss of consideration, one that acknowledged their shared space and the unusual circumstances that had brought them together. Then, his gaze flickered to Elena, a fleeting, almost imperceptible glance that held no invitation, no challenge, just a neutral acknowledgment of her presence.

Then, the kiss deepened. The sweetness intensified, blossoming into something more. It was a kiss of longing, of connection, of a desire that had been simmering beneath the surface. His hands found her waist, pulling her closer, molding their bodies together. Tanya responded, her initial hesitation melting away like snow in the Texas sun. The chamomile tea was forgotten, resting on the counter as her arms wrapped around his neck.

Elena watched, an unreadable expression on her face. There was no jealousy, no anger, perhaps a flicker of... amusement? Or maybe even a touch of wistfulness? It was hard to tell with Elena. She was a master of disguise. David, lost in the moment, barely registered Elena's presence. He was focused solely on Tanya, on the feel of her skin beneath his hands, the taste of her lips, the way she leaned into him, abandoning herself to the kiss. He was careful, methodical, yet passionate, each touch deliberate, each movement designed to heighten her pleasure.

Slowly, deliberately, he began to undress her. First, the soft, worn t-shirt she often slept in, lifting it over her head with a gentle tug. Then, the comfortable sweatpants, sliding them down her legs, revealing the smooth, tanned skin beneath. He paused, his eyes meeting hers, a silent question in their depths. Tanya responded with a soft sigh and a barely perceptible nod.

He continued, his movements unhurried, reverent. He unclasped her bra, allowing it to fall to the floor. He kissed her again, his lips trailing down her neck, her chest, his hands tracing the curves of her body. Elena remained at the counter, seemingly engrossed in her manicure, but David knew she was watching. He didn't care.

As Tanya stood before him, naked and vulnerable, David felt a surge of protectiveness. He held Tanya against the cool granite countertop. He pulled away from the kiss, just enough to catch his breath, his gaze locking with Tanya's. Her eyes were wide, dilated, reflecting the dim light of the kitchen. He saw vulnerability, but also a raw desire that mirrored his own.

He reached down, tugging at the drawstring of his pajama pants. They fell silently to the floor. Tanya gasped softly, her hands tightening on his shoulders. He kissed her again, deeper this time, a primal urgency fueling the connection. He pressed his body against hers, the cool countertop a stark contrast to the heat that flared between them.

With a deft movement, she guided him, pulling him into her. A low moan escaped her lips, a sound that resonated deep within David's chest. He braced his hands on the counter, supporting his weight as he moved within her. The world narrowed, there was only Tanya, the feel of her body against his, the frantic rhythm of their breaths. Elena remained a silent observer, a splash of color in the drab kitchen. He saw her reflection in the stainless steel appliances, her head tilted slightly, as if analyzing the performance.

Tanya's fingernails dug into his back as she met his thrusts with a fierce abandon. Her hips bucked against him, her breath coming in ragged gasps. He could feel her tightening around him, pulling him deeper, urging him on. It was raw, uninhibited, a desperate release from the tension that had been building since the blackout. The scent of chamomile, mingled with the earthy aroma of sex, filled the air. It was a strange, almost comical juxtaposition. He imagined Lynn, Josh's overbearing mother, catching a whiff of the scene. The woman would probably faint. He smiled inwardly at the thought.

Faster now, harder, he felt the edge approaching. His muscles tensed, his vision blurring. He heard Tanya cry out, her body arching against him. He closed his eyes, surrendering to the overwhelming pleasure. A quiet roar escaped his lips as he reached his peak, his body convulsing with release. The aftermath was a slow descent back to reality. He rested his forehead against Tanya's shoulder, his breath ragged. She wrapped her arms around him, holding him tight.

After a few moments, he pulled away, reluctantly breaking the connection. He looked down at Tanya, her face flushed, her hair disheveled. She smiled weakly. "Wow," she whispered, her voice hoarse. "Yeah," he agreed, a rare hint of genuine emotion in his voice. "Wow." He stepped back, retrieving his pajama pants from the floor. He pulled them on, feeling the cool fabric against his skin. He turned to Elena, who was now meticulously examining her nails. "Well, that was… stimulating," she said, her voice dry. "Perhaps we should all take a cold shower." Tanya kissed David one last time before picking up her clothes and scurrying off. David then smiled wickedly at Elena, then grabbed her by the hips, pulling her toward him. Elena chuckled, a low, throaty sound that hinted at the amusement she always seemed to find in David's antics. "David, darling, you're insatiable. But I suppose that's one of your many… charms."

He grinned, his eyes sparkling with mischief. "And you find me charming, admit it." He pulled her closer, the cool tile of the kitchen floor a stark contrast to the heat radiating from her body. "Charming in a 'this might be the last night of civilization, and I need a distraction' kind of way? Perhaps." She raised a perfectly sculpted eyebrow. "But then again, any port in a storm, wouldn't you agree?"

He nipped playfully at her ear. "Ouch, Elena, you wound me deeply! I thought we had something special. You know, besides the impending societal collapse and the copious amounts of stored peanut butter." "Oh, we do," she purred, wrapping her arms around his neck. "I have a profound appreciation for your… dedication to procreation. And let's not forget your rather impressive intellectual capacity. You're like a walking, talking, breeding supercomputer. What's not to love?"

83

David laughed, a genuine, hearty sound. "You know just how to inflate a guy's ego." He leaned in, his lips brushing against hers. "So, about that cold shower…" "Later," she breathed, pulling him closer. "Right now, I'm thinking we need to conduct a more… thorough quality control assessment."

Chapter 6

The Final Word

The aroma of fresh waffles mingled with the distinct scent of David's meticulously brewed coffee. "Right, operation 'Get Lynn Some Decent Clothes' is a go," David announced, his voice cutting through the morning fog. He tapped a pen against a notepad, his expression a blend of seriousness and thinly veiled exasperation. "We've all noticed Lynn has been 'borrowing' clothes from the closet, and considering you ladies have a certain… je-ne-sais-quoi that Lynn seems to lack, it's not exactly a flattering look."

A wave of stifled giggles rippled through the women. Jennifer, never one to miss an opportunity for a playful jab, piped up, "Well, Master, it's hard to rock Tiffany's yoga pants when you're, shall we say, built for comfort, not speed?" "Don't start, Jen," David sighed, though a hint of a smile played on his lips. "The point is, it's time for a shopping trip. Josh," he turned his attention to Lily's perpetually bewildered-looking husband, who was nervously picking at his breakfast. "You're on point for this one."

Josh swallowed hard. "Me? Shopping? With my mom?" "Exactly," David said, his tone leaving no room for argument. "She's your mother, and besides… It's good for experience. Now," David continued, "you have two options. You either drive 100 miles to Lynn's place and drop her off, or you brave

Austin, which is only 50 miles, but guaranteed to be a chaotic mess." He paused. "Personally, I'm leaning towards the 'abandon Lynn in the wilderness' option, but the wives are against it."

A chorus of "David!" erupted from the women, punctuated by Jessica's indignant gasp. "Daddy!" "Alright, alright," David conceded, holding up his hands in mock surrender. "Austin it is. Aidan," he called out to his eldest son. "Saddle up your propane-powered beast. They need transportation."

Summer spoke up. "David, dear, perhaps we should send someone else along as security? Just in case Austin is as bad as we think it will be." A wave of hands shot up around the table. Before he could make a decision, a small but determined voice piped up. "I want to go with Josh!"

All eyes turned to Lily. She stood tall, a miniature version of her father, her eyes sparkling with determination. "Lily, honey, are you sure?" Summer asked, concerned. "It could be dangerous." "I can handle it, Mom," Lily insisted. "Besides, Josh is my husband, and I've seen what's out there."

David studied his daughter, a proud grin spreading across his face. "Alright, Lily. You're in. You're the security detail. Make sure Josh doesn't wander off and gets Lynn the right sizes!" "Yes, Daddy!" Lily squealed, beaming. "Okay, so, Josh, Lily, and Aidan are going to Austin with Lynn, I expect you to be back before sunset, under no circumstance should we be using the NVGs." David said, his tone serious.

The scene in the garage was bordering on farcical. There was Aidan, looking like a futuristic chauffeur in his tactical vest, lifting his car out of the depths of storage on the cable lift, while a cherry-red beast that somehow managed to look both menacing and environmentally conscious appeared out of the ground. Lily, small but fierce, was meticulously checking the magazines on her P365, her M4 slung to her front. Josh, on the other hand, fumbled as he holstered his Sig P226 in a drop leg holster. "Are you sure you know what to do, Josh?" Aidan asked, not unkindly. Josh gulped. "I think I have enough practice... for a test run at least."

Lynn, meanwhile, was having a full-blown meltdown. "I am not wearing that thing!" she declared, gesturing to the bulky ballistic vest Aidan was trying to hand her. "It's uncomfortable! And what if someone shoots me in the face?" David, who had followed them to the garage, pinched the bridge of his nose. "Lynn, it's not supposed to be comfortable. It's body armor. There are... unpleasant people out there. People who might want to... take your purse, or worse." "But it's so bulky!" Lynn whined, throwing her hands up in exasperation. "I'll look like a turtle waddling through the mall! Nobody wears body armor on shopping trips!" "Mom," Josh interjected, trying to reason with her. "Things are different now. We need to be careful."

Lynn glared at him. "Don't 'Mom' me, Joshua! You're starting to sound just like your father-in-law. And I still haven't recovered from seeing that man kill those boys with a sword!" She shuddered, the memory of David's brutal efficiency clearly still haunting her. David chose to ignore the comment. He knew Lynn was still processing the change in the world, and the necessary violence it sometimes demanded. "Look, Lynn," he said, his voice softening. "Just consider it a very sturdy, very unattractive purse. It holds all your vital organs. Please?" Seeing the imploring look on David's face, and the determined look in Lily's eyes, Lynn finally relented. "Fine," she grumbled, allowing Aidan to help her into the vest. "But if I get any weird looks at Nordstrom, I'm blaming all of you."

With Lynn reluctantly armored up, and Josh still looking slightly worried, the four piled into the beast. Aidan revved the engine, the sound a surprisingly tame purr thanks to the propane conversion. Lily hopped into the passenger seat, her M4 resting comfortably across her lap. Josh squeezed into the back with Lynn, the Sig P226 digging uncomfortably into his thigh.

As they pulled out of the driveway, David watched them go, a mixture of amusement and concern on his face. He knew Aidan and Lily could handle themselves, but Josh and Lynn were a different story. He just hoped "Operation: Get Lynn Some Decent Clothes" wouldn't turn into "Operation: Rescue Josh and Lynn from a Fashion-Fueled Apocalypse."

The drive to Austin was surprisingly uneventful. The highways were still littered with abandoned cars, monuments to the sudden blackout that had crippled the world, but Aidan navigated the obstacles like a pro. Lily kept a watchful eye on the surroundings, her senses on high alert. Josh, meanwhile, spent most of the journey staring quietly out the window.

As they neared Austin, the signs of civilization became more apparent. Some businesses were open, some remained closed. People were walking the streets, some armed, some simply trying to maintain a semblance of normalcy. Aidan pulled up to a department store that looked surprisingly unscathed. "Alright, let's do this quickly," he said, his voice serious. "Grab what you need and get out." Lily nodded in agreement. "Josh, you stick with Lynn. I'll be watching our backs."

Stepping into the store was like stepping back in time. The shelves were still stocked, the mannequins still posed in fashionable outfits. But the air was thick with a sense of unease. Lynn, suddenly gasped. "I don't have very much money," she said, as if suddenly realizing commerce was a thing. Lily waved her hand dismissively. "Daddy has plenty, just try and limit it to what you can cram into two duffel bags." Josh trailed behind her, looking increasingly overwhelmed. He had never been much of a shopper, and the sheer volume of clothing was making his head spin.

As Lynn and Josh disappeared into the store, Lily took up her position just inside the entrance, a silent guardian. The air inside was thick with the scent of perfume and unfulfilled consumer desires. The silence was broken only by the faint murmur of customers and the distant echo of heels on the polished floor.

She noticed them immediately. Three men, leaning against a display case near the men's department, their eyes tracking her every move. They were the wrong kind of clean, their too-casual posture radiating a predatory energy. They had that "we're trying to look innocent but failing miserably" vibe that screamed trouble. Lily subtly brought her hand to her ear, activating her comm. "Aidan, we have company. Three males, approximate age 20s-30s, watching us. Keep an eye out." "Roger that," Aidan's voice crackled in her ear. "I'm adjusting the vehicle's position. Stay sharp."

Inside the store, Lynn was in her element. She flitted between racks of dresses, her fingers caressing the fabrics. Josh, meanwhile, trailed behind her, his face a mask of apprehension. "Mom, maybe we should hurry?" he whispered, tugging at her sleeve. "Lily said we only have thirty minutes." "Oh, Joshua, relax," Lynn said, waving him off. "A good dress sale waits for no one. Besides," she added, lowering her voice conspiratorially, "with everything that's going on, these clothes are practically free!"

As Lynn squealed with delight over a particularly gaudy sequined top, Josh caught Lily's eye. She gave him a subtle nod, a silent reassurance that she was on guard. He managed a weak smile in return, grateful for her presence. Lynn, oblivious to the undercurrent of tension, continued her shopping spree. She filled a shopping cart with dresses, blouses, shoes, and handbags, chattering incessantly about her "finds."

Finally, after what felt like an eternity, Lynn declared herself satisfied. "Alright, Joshua, let's get these treasures back to the car." As they approached the exit, Lily stepped forward, her hand resting on her weapon. The three men had moved closer, blocking their path. "Well, well, well," one of the men said, his voice dripping with false charm. "Look what we have here. Aren't you a feisty little lamb."

Lily's eyes narrowed. "Step aside," she said, her voice cold and hard. "We don't want any trouble." The man chuckled. "We don't want any trouble either, little girl. But you folks look like you're out of your element, how about we give you a hand?" He gestured to the shopping cart.

Lily didn't hesitate. In one swift motion, she drew her pistol, aiming it at the man speaking. "I said, step aside," she repeated, her voice even colder than before. The men froze, their bravado momentarily deflated by the sight of the gun. But only momentarily. "You think a little pop gun is going to scare us?" one of them sneered. "There's three of us and only one of you." "Don't be so sure about that," a voice said from behind them.

The men turned to see Josh, his face pale but determined, brandishing his Sig P226. "This kid looks scared to death," one of the men chuckled. "And don't forget about me," Lynn announced, brandishing a high-heeled shoe like a weapon. "I may be older, but I can still pack a punch." Lily almost choked on a laugh. Leave it to Lynn to turn a potential firefight into a bizarre comedy routine.

But the levity didn't last. The men, realizing they were outnumbered and outgunned (slightly), decided to retreat. "This isn't over," one of them snarled. "We'll be seeing you again." They turned and fled, disappearing into the maze of clothing racks. Lily watched them go, her eyes narrowed with suspicion. "Let's go," she said, herding Lynn and Josh towards the exit. "We need to get out of here." As they emerged from the store, Aidan was waiting for them, the "car" idling menacingly.

He took one look at Lily's face and knew something had gone down. "What happened?" he asked, his voice laced with concern. "We had some unwanted admirers," Lily said. "They backed off, but I don't think we've seen the last of them. Let's get back to the house, now." As they pulled away from the department store, Lily glanced back, her eyes scanning the shadows.

As they left the shopping center, a gold Suburban slowly followed. On the highway, Aidan gripped the wheel, his knuckles white. He glanced in the rearview mirror. The gold Suburban was still there, glued to their tail. "We're being followed," Lily stated, her voice calm but sharp. "I noticed," Aidan replied, his eyes flicking between the road and the mirror. "They're trying to push me. I could outrun them, but I don't want them knowing where we live." Lily nodded, understanding flashing in her eyes. "Then we make a stand. Find a good spot."

Aidan scanned the surroundings. The highway was flanked by a desolate, scrub-filled landscape. He spotted a wide, empty turnout up ahead, a place where truckers probably used to take breaks before the blackout. "There," he pointed. "That'll do." He signaled, expertly downshifted, and pulled the muscle car into the turnout. The Suburban screeched to a halt behind them, kicking up a cloud of dust and gravel. Five men piled out, their faces hard and menacing. "Stay here," Lily ordered, her voice unexpectedly sweet. She reached under the seat, pulling out her M4. Josh, and Lynn, despite her initial shock, knew the drill. They huddled down, out of sight.

Lily stepped out of the car, the M4 held loosely but ready. "What do you want?" she called out, her voice calm and steady. "We want what's yours," the apparent leader of the group sneered, stepping forward. He was a burly man with a greasy beard and a cruel glint in his eyes. "That car, those guns...and maybe you too."

Lily's eyes narrowed. "You're welcome to try," she said, her voice dangerously soft. The leader laughed, a harsh, grating sound. "You're just one little girl. You think you can take us all on?" "I'm not alone," Lily replied, her eyes flicking towards the car. The leader scoffed. "Looks like you're all alone to me." He gestured to his men, and they began to fan out, flanking Lily. Lily raised her M4. "You're making a mistake."

Before the leader could respond, a high-pitched whine filled the air. It was the unmistakable sound of the muscle car's propane engine spooling up, but not in the way they expected. Aidan had reconfigured the exhaust system with a valve and nozzles. Aidan opened the valve, releasing a jet of propane directly into the exhaust. With a deafening roar, the car erupted in flames, a massive gout of fire spewing from the pipes just to the side of where the 'leader' was standing.

The men recoiled in surprise and fear, momentarily stunned by the unexpected attack. Lily used the distraction to her advantage. She shouldered the M4 and fired two controlled bursts, each aimed at the legs of the men closest to her. They screamed and went down, clutching their wounded limbs.

The leader, momentarily blinded by the flames, roared in rage. He pulled a pistol from his waistband and before he could shoot, two shots hit him in the abdomen. "Josh, now!" Lily yelled from outside the car. Josh, his initial fear replaced by a surge of adrenaline, kicked the door open. Knocking the man onto the ground as the door slammed into him.

Aidan emerged from the driver's seat, and after removing the man's pistol from his hand, pointed it at the others. "That's enough," he said, his voice cold and hard. "Get in your car and leave. Now." The remaining two men, seeing their leader wounded and their comrades incapacitated, didn't need any further encouragement. They scrambled back into the Suburban and sped away, leaving a trail of dust and wounded pride in their wake.

Lily watched them go, her heart pounding in her chest. She lowered her M4 and took a deep breath. The silence that followed was deafening. "Everyone okay?" she asked, her voice surprisingly calm. "I'm fine," Aidan said, reaching down to pick up the man, still disoriented, and bleeding from his abdomen. "Josh did good." Josh blushed, but a small smile played on his lips. "Thanks."

Even Lynn, despite her earlier anxieties, seemed impressed. "Well, I'll be," she muttered. "You kids are something else." Lily turned her attention to the wounded men on the ground. She approached them cautiously, her M4 still at the ready. "Don't move," she ordered. "I'm not going to kill you, but I'm not going to let you cause any more trouble either."

As Josh shakily provided cover, she quickly assessed their injuries. The wounds were serious, but not life-threatening. She pulled out a roll of bandages from her backpack and began to administer first aid. "Why are you helping us?" one of the wounded men groaned. "We were trying to hurt you." Aidan shrugged, unceremoniously sticking a knife into the leader's carotid artery. "That doesn't mean we're going to let you die. Besides," he added with a wry smile, "Unless you want to end up like him, you'll take heed."

Once they were finished, Aidan stood up and surveyed the scene. The car was still smoldering, but the fire was slowly dying down. The gold Suburban was long gone. The air was thick with the smell of blood, smoke, and fear. "Let's get out of here," he said, his voice grim. "This place gives me the creeps."

They piled back into the car, leaving the wounded men to their fate. Aidan started the engine and pulled back onto the highway, heading back towards the sanctuary of their home. As they drove, Lily leaned over and squeezed Josh's hand. "You were amazing," she said, her eyes filled with pride.

As Aidan steered the muscle car into the driveway. Little David, ever vigilant, remotely activated the heavy steel door of the garage, allowing Aidan to guide the vehicle onto the cable lift platform. The scent of burnt propane still clung to the air. Lynn, her face pale and drawn, practically tumbled out of the back seat. Josh, usually cheerful and optimistic, wore a somber expression.

He watched as Aidan efficiently shut down the engine and engaged the lift's safety mechanisms. "Aidan," Josh began tentatively, his voice barely audible. "Why... why did you kill that guy? The leader? Lily patched up the other two." Aidan turned, his face betraying nothing. His gaze, usually warm and friendly, was now as cold and hard as the concrete walls surrounding them. He paused, considering his words carefully, a trait he undoubtedly inherited from his father. "Lily did her best," Aidan said, his voice flat. "But he was beyond help. The wounds he sustained, internal damage... he wouldn't have made it." Josh looked at Aidan sympathetically. "Mercy?"

Lily, who had been silently inspecting her M4, stepped into the conversation. "Josh," she said softly, her voice carrying an undercurrent of steel that belied her youthful appearance. "Aidan made the right call. We don't have the resources to play doctor for every low life who tries to take what's ours. Besides..." she paused, her gaze hardening. "He wanted to... take me. He made his choice when he stepped out of that Suburban." Josh visibly flinched at her words, understanding dawning in his eyes. Without another word, he reached out, embracing Lily.

Lynn, who had been silently observing the exchange, finally spoke, her voice laced with disapproval. "Really, Aidan? Was that necessary? We could have just left them there. Killing... It's barbaric." Aidan's jaw tightened, but he held his tongue. He knew arguing with Lynn was a futile exercise. Her overprotective nature, amplified by the chaos of the world, grated on his nerves. He respected her as Josh's mother, but her constant criticism and refusal to grasp the realities of their situation were wearing thin. He then realized that David's dislike of her was becoming increasingly understandable.

Lily, sensing the tension, stepped forward and placed a hand on Aidan's arm. Her touch was light but reassuring. "Let's go inside," she said, her voice gentle but firm. "We need to debrief with Dad and Summer." As they moved towards the stairs, leaving Lynn to grumble about the dangers of violence, little David activated the lift, sending the red monster back into the depths of the storage bunker.

Aidan, Lily, then Josh walked into the upper hallway, meeting David on his way into the dining room. "How did it go?" he asked, his voice calm but authoritative. Lily recounted their shopping trip, the encounter in the department store, and the pursuit on the highway. She described Aidan's quick thinking, Josh's bravery, and the difficult decision Aidan had made.

David listened intently, his expression betraying nothing. When she finished, he nodded slowly, his gaze shifting to Aidan. "You did what you had to do," he said, his voice firm but devoid of judgment. "This world doesn't reward hesitation. It rewards decisive action." He turned to Josh, his gaze softening slightly. "You did well too, Josh. It's not easy to face violence, especially when you're not used to it. But you stood your ground. That takes courage."

As Lynn fumbled upstairs, David had an idea. "Summer, get everybody into the living room for an emergency meeting," he commanded, his eyes still fixed on

Lynn. As the entire family gathered, David looked across the room. His nine wives, his six children, his two daughters-in-law, his son-in-law, his brother-in-law, and his son-in-law's mother.

"Thank you all for coming," he began, his voice calm and steady, a stark contrast to the turmoil churning inside him. "As you know, the situation outside is deteriorating. The blackout was just the beginning. Things are going to get significantly worse." He paused, his blue eyes, usually filled with warmth, now held a steely gaze. "I'm sick and tired of the lack of cooperation. Some of you still haven't grasped the severity of our situation." His gaze flickered towards Lynn, whose lips tightened into a thin line. "We have a responsibility here," David continued, his voice gaining intensity. "A responsibility to each other, and to the future. This isn't a game. This isn't a temporary inconvenience. This is about survival."

He rose from his chair, pacing slowly in front of the fireplace. "There are twenty of us in this room. Twenty people living within the protective walls of everything we have built together through the years." He swept his hand, encompassing them all. "In a way, we are a microcosm of the entire planet." A murmur rippled through the room. Tiffany nodded her head, a silent affirmation of her understanding.

David stopped pacing, his gaze fixed on the floor. "The power will fail again. It's not a question of if, but when. The climate will become more erratic, more dangerous. The water sources will be tainted, poisoned by the dead and decaying." He looked up, his eyes meeting theirs, one by one. "More people will die. A lot more."

He took a deep breath. "I need you all to understand something crucial. If this room represents the entire population of the planet, and with how things are going, then in seven years…" He paused, letting the weight of his words hang in the air. "…the only person who will be left alive will be the baby." He pointed towards Jessica, who instinctively placed a hand on her slightly rounded stomach. Her eyes widened, fear momentarily eclipsing the usual calm serenity that radiated from her.

He saw the fear in Lynn's eyes, the panic barely concealed beneath her overbearing mother hen facade. Good. Let her be afraid. Fear was a motivator, and she desperately needed motivation to cooperate. He broke the silence. "I want to be perfectly clear," David said, his voice resonating with authority. "I am not a prophet. I have no delusions of grandeur. I am a pragmatist. I see patterns, I analyze data, and I draw conclusions. My conclusions, based on my… unique perspective, are grim."

He paused again, his gaze sweeping the room. "I have spent decades preparing for this. Stockpiling resources, building defenses, training you all. Not because I wanted to play warlord, but because I knew, on a fundamental level, that this was coming. This is not some prepper fantasy, this is cold, hard reality."

Kayla finally spoke, her voice measured. "David, are you saying that you truly believe that within seven years, everyone outside this house will be dead?" "Essentially, yes," he replied, his eyes meeting hers. "The blackout was just the catalyst. The collapse will be cascading. Famine, disease, civil unrest... it will all feed on itself until there's nothing left but pockets of survivors clinging to existence, fighting over scraps."

Lynn scoffed, "That's ridiculous! The government will restore order. FEMA will..." David cut her off, his voice sharp. "FEMA is already overwhelmed. The government is fractured and collapsing. There is no cavalry coming. We... are the cavalry."

He walked to the window, peering out at the darkening landscape. "I have no illusions about the kind of choices we will have to make," he continued, his voice low. "Survival will demand sacrifices. Compromises. Things that will test the very limits of our humanity." He turned back to face them. "I am not going to sugarcoat this. I am not going to pretend that everything will be alright. Because it won't. It will be brutal. It will be ugly. And it will be constant."

He took a deep breath, his gaze hardening. "My priority is the survival of my family. My wives. My children. My grandchildren. And those who have proven their loyalty and commitment to this community." He leveled his gaze directly at Lynn. "If you contribute, if you follow my instructions, if you put the needs of the group above your own selfish desires, then you will be protected. But if you undermine me, if you sow discord, if you prioritize your own comfort over the safety of everyone else... then you are a liability. And I will deal with liabilities accordingly."

His words hung in the air, cold and unforgiving. He saw the defiance flicker in Lynn's eyes, but he also saw a glimmer of fear. Good. Let her understand the stakes. "This is not a democracy," he continued, his voice unwavering. "This is a survival initiative. I am the leader. My decisions are final. If you have a problem with that, or if you don't like my methods, then get the fuck out."

He paused, letting his words sink in. "I am not obligated to take care of any of you. I have my hands full protecting my own family. However, I will take care of what belongs to me, whoever readily submits to the community in order to be protected by me." He made eye contact with each of his wives, a silent message passing between them. They understood. They had chosen this life. They had surrendered to his leadership, his vision, his… dominance.

He walked over to Jessica and knelt beside her, placing a hand gently on her stomach. "And as for you, little one," he said softly, "you are the future. You are the reason we are fighting. And I will do everything in my power to protect you." He gave Luci a scratch behind the ears before rising. The cat purred softly, seemingly unfazed by the tension in the room. "Since there are no questions, I suggest you think about what I said." Without another word, David dismissed the group.

Chapter 7

Welcoming the Newcomers

David stepped onto the porch, the afternoon sun warm on his face. He adjusted the Beretta on his hip, a habit more than a necessity. Eighteen family members, a veritable armed escort, fanned out behind him, a silent testament to preparedness. He could practically hear Jessica rolling her eyes from inside, probably muttering something about being "extra." He knew it was a bit much, but frankly, he enjoyed the display. It was good for morale, and it certainly got the point across.

As the three unexpected vehicles parked on the edge of the property line, Parker, Eric, and a slightly bewildered Scott, three of the five soldiers he met nineteen years ago, climbed out of their vehicles, looking road-weary and apprehensive. Parker was the first to speak. "David, good to see you. Figured this would be the best place to ride out whatever's happening." His gruff voice held a hint of desperation, barely masked by his usual stoicism.

Eric, lean and wiry, nodded in agreement. "Yeah, things are getting hairy out there. We remembered your place, and well, we hoped you might have room for us." His young daughter, Bonnie, peeked out from behind his leg, clutching a tattered doll. Scott, wide-eyed, just stared at the armed contingent surrounding David's house. Andrea, his wife, gave his arm a gentle squeeze, and his son, Mike, looked around with nervous curiosity. "David? It's... been a while."

David, his expression neutral, offered a small, almost imperceptible smile. "Parker, Eric. Good to see you both. Scott, it has been a long time. Welcome. It's... fortuitous that you remembered us." He paused, his gaze sweeping over the families, taking in their exhaustion and the obvious strain. "Come on in. Let's get you all settled." He gestured towards the house, deliberately avoiding any mention of the expansive underground complex beneath their feet. Let them assume the worst – garage floors and barnyard accommodations. It would make the eventual reveal all the more satisfying.

Tiffany, ever the gracious hostess, stepped forward, hugging Jill, Parker's wife and Andrea. "Come on, everyone. We have plenty of food and drinks. Let's get you fed and cleaned up." She ushered Andrea, Jill, Mike and Bonnie towards the house, her maternal instincts kicking into high gear. Summer followed close behind. Jennifer, never one to miss an opportunity, sauntered up to David. "Master, should I prepare them rooms?" She batted her eyelashes, a playful look in her eyes. David suppressed a chuckle. "Go prepare the first three apartments, but do it quietly."

Parker, Eric, and Scott exchanged confused glances. This wasn't exactly the rustic, survivalist compound they had envisioned. It was... a bizarre blend of hospitality, military precision, and domesticity, seasoned with a healthy dose of the surreal. "So," Parker drawled, turning to David, "It looks like your family's grown a bit." David smiled, looking at his wives as they brought out drinks. David returned Parker's knowing smile. "Indeed it has. Pull up a chair, let's talk." He gestured towards the back deck, where Tiffany had already set up lemonade and cookies.

As they settled into the patio chairs, David's expression turned serious. "So, what brings you all the way out here? I know you didn't just stumble upon us by chance." He looked pointedly at Parker and Eric, who exchanged a knowing glance. "Especially you two. You know how well-stocked we are. And you're eighty miles away. That's a long drive with the roads as they are now."

Parker sighed, running a hand through his hair. "Okay, you got us. Truth is, things are getting real bad out there, even with the power coming back. It just keeps getting worse, and we realized, we weren't as prepared as we thought we were." He paused, choosing his words carefully. "We saw the blackout, the chaos... and we remembered you. Remembered what you always said about being ready. Figured this was the only place that would be."

Eric nodded in agreement. "My place got ransacked. People are desperate. Bonnie and I barely made it out." He hugged his daughter tighter, his eyes filled with a simmering anger. Scott, looking increasingly uncomfortable, chimed in, "Andrea and I... we just want to keep Mike safe. We have a little bit of food and water, but it won't last. We hoped you would be able to help." "I understand," he said finally. "But you need to understand something too. This isn't a hotel. We have rules, we have a system. We work together. We survive together."

Eric cut to the chase. "What do you expect from us, David? What's the price of admission?" David leaned forward, his gaze unwavering. "Loyalty. Hard work. Commitment. Trust." He paused for emphasis. "Those are the cornerstones of this community. You disrespect those, you disrespect us all. And you won't be welcome here." He continued, "Parker, Eric, I know you both. I know your skills, your dedication. Scott, I remember you, but things have changed. So, let me be clear. Everyone contributes here. Everyone pulls their weight. We have a schedule, duties, training. This isn't some free-for-all FEMA shelter. This is a highly structured, self-sufficient family. My family. Can you handle that?"

"Alright," he continued, his voice calm and authoritative. "Welcome. You all know the situation outside is… less than ideal. Here, we're self-sufficient. You're safe. Consider this a haven." He paused, his eyes flicking to each person, ensuring they understood the gravity of his words. "Relax. Get settled. You've earned it." He turned to Tiffany, a silent command passing between them. "Tiffany, could you give Jill, Andrea, Mike, and Bonnie a tour of the barn? They might find it… interesting." A slight smile played on his lips, knowing the reactions the miniature cows were sure to elicit.

Next, he focused on his sons. "Aidan, David, you two take Parker, Eric, and Scott to the shooting range, then show them the work shed. Let them see what we're working with." He deliberately omitted any mention of the bunkers. They would learn about those in due time, but for now, compartmentalization was key. As the groups dispersed,

David felt a familiar sense of satisfaction. Control. Organization. He watched as Tiffany led her group through the house. Aidan and David Jr., ever eager, were already leading the veterans towards the back of the property.

Later, as the sun reached its zenith, the tour groups began to trickle back. Jill and Andrea were practically buzzing with excitement, their faces flushed with wonder. "David," Jill began, her voice animated, "that barn is amazing! The cows are... miniature! I've never seen anything like it!" Andrea nodded enthusiastically. "The whole thing is so... efficient. And clean! You've really thought of everything." Mike, usually shy, tugged on his mother's sleeve, his eyes wide. "Mom, can we get a tiny cow? Please?" Bonnie, still clinging to Eric, peeked out from behind his leg, a small smile gracing her lips. Clearly, the miniature cows had made an impression on her as well.

Parker, Eric, and Scott approached, a mixture of awe and professional assessment on their faces. "Impressive setup, David," Parker said, his voice laced with respect. "The range is well-maintained, and that work shed... you've got some serious equipment there. Kyle's a wizard with those guns." Scott, however, had a more direct question. "So, where do we clean up?" he asked, pulling at his jacket. David simply smiled enigmatically, offering no further explanation. He enjoyed the speculation. The mystery. He preferred to reveal information on his own terms. "Dinner will be at five thirty," he announced, changing the subject. "Plenty of time to get cleaned up."

David led the newly arrived group towards the garage. Dust swirled around their feet, kicked up from the parched earth. David kept a watchful eye on them, cataloging their expressions and movements. Tiffany, ever the observant leader, and Jennifer, ever the playful instigator, flanked him, their presence a silent assurance. "Alright," David announced, his voice clear and concise, cutting through the relative silence. "This is the garage. Half underground, reinforced. For now, you can leave your stuff in here, and wash up – dinner will be in a couple of hours."

He pressed a button on the wall, and the heavy steel door of the garage rumbled open, revealing a surprisingly spacious interior. Parker, Jill, Eric, Bonnie, Scott, Andrea, and Mike shuffled inside, their eyes wide as they took in the meticulously organized space, the massive lift in front of the door, and the three doors. David pointed to the stairs to his right. "Those go up to the house, so if we have meetings or gatherings, you don't have to go outside."

David opened the door to his left, revealing a long hallway with multiple doors, each leading to a room. "Each room is equipped with the essentials," David explained, gesturing with a sweep of his hand. "Queen sized bed, clean linens, climate control and a desk. There are three bathrooms, two in this portion, along with a communal kitchen and dining room. Make yourselves comfortable."

The guests dispersed, tentatively opening doors and stepping into the guest rooms. Jill peeked into one, a silent gasp escaping her lips. The LCD screen window displayed a vibrant forest scene, complete with birdsong and the rustling of leaves. It wasn't a real window, but it was far better than the grim reality they'd left behind.

Bonnie, Eric's daughter, skipped into the room, her eyes fixated on the "window." "Daddy, look! It's like we're in a real forest!" Eric picked up the remote, flicking through the scenes, until he came across a dark pasture. As he unpacked, Bonnie shrieked. "Daddy, zombies!" she screamed, before hiding under the blanket. The display was a realistic zombie horde, trying to break in through the window.

In another room, Parker ran a hand over the smooth, cool surface of the wall, a flicker of something akin to hope in his eyes. He knew quality work when he saw it, and it was clear David had put a lot of thought and effort into this place. "They seem…relieved," Tiffany observed, her gaze sweeping over the garage doors. "Relieved is an understatement," Jennifer chuckled. "They look like they've won the lottery." David nodded. "Relief is temporary. Commitment is what matters." He paused, his gaze fixed on the horizon. "Come dinner, we'll see who's truly willing to adapt."

Later, the aroma of roasted chicken and mashed potatoes filled the air. The dining room, a long, sturdy table was buzzing with conversation. Kayla and Tanya, with their culinary skills, had worked tirelessly to prepare a feast. Summer oversaw the table setting with her usual precision, ensuring every detail was perfect.

Parker, ever the polite guest, raised his glass. "To David, for his generosity and hospitality." Everyone echoed his sentiment. "This is an amazing property, David," Scott said, admiring the solid construction of the house. "You've really thought of everything." Andrea nodded in agreement. "And the land is beautiful. We wouldn't mind helping out with chores, pulling our weight." Others chimed in, echoing their willingness to contribute. Eric offered his military expertise, Jill her nursing skills, and Scott his knowledge of construction. Mike, Scott's son, piped up enthusiastically, "I can help with the animals!"

David listened patiently, his expression unchanged. Once the enthusiastic offers subsided, he cleared his throat. The room fell silent, all eyes on him. "I appreciate your willingness to help," he began, his voice calm but firm. "However, I want to be perfectly clear about something." He paused, letting his words hang in the air. "I have no intention of accommodating 'guests' here." A collective murmur rippled through the room. Parker frowned, and Eric crossed his arms, his eyes narrowed.

David continued, his gaze sweeping across each face. "What I offer here is not just shelter and food. It's a way of life. A commitment to building something lasting." He leaned forward, his intensity palpable. "If you choose to stay here, you will become part of my family. You will adhere to my rules, contribute to our collective survival, and dedicate yourselves to our shared future."

He paused again, allowing his words to sink in. "I need to know if you are prepared to make that commitment. Are you willing to fully integrate? Are you willing to become something more?" The cheerful atmosphere of a moment ago was gone, replaced by a palpable tension. David watched them carefully, searching for honesty, commitment, and an understanding of what he was offering. He knew that genuine integration was the key to the survival of his family. The world outside was in chaos, and he needed to build more than just a refuge, he needed to create a community, a force that can face anything.

The silence stretched, punctuated only by the clinking of forks against the plates. David, usually impatient, waited with deliberate calm. He knew this wasn't a decision to be rushed. He was offering them a chance, not demanding their servitude. He saw the fear in their eyes, the uncertainty, but also a glimmer of something else – hope.

Parker, ever the leader, was the first to break the silence. He straightened his posture, the soldier in him re-emerging. "David," he said, his voice rough, "we came here looking for safety. But you're offering something more than that. You're offering purpose. I'm in." Jill nodded, squeezing Parker's hand. "We're a team. If he's in, I'm in."

Eric, his shoulders slumping slightly, looked at his daughter, Bonnie. He saw the fear still lingering in her eyes, but also a flicker of excitement. "For Bonnie," he said quietly, "I'm in." Scott and Andrea exchanged a look. Andrea spoke first, "We want to protect our son. We are in this together." Mike, who was busy playing with one of the dachshunds near their feet, suddenly looked up, "I want to help with the animals."

David tilted his head slightly, a hint of a smile playing on his lips. "Very well," he said. "Then welcome to the family." The tension in the room eased, replaced by a sense of cautious optimism. David stood and gestured towards the

French doors. "Now that I have your pledge of loyalty, how about a tour?"

The confused murmurs rippled through the group. Parker frowned, scratching his head. "Didn't your wife already show us the barn, David?" David held up a hand, his expression both patient and firm. "That was a preliminary welcome. Now that you're family, there are... deeper levels of understanding required. The safety of this entire property, everyone within it, now rests partly on your shoulders. That requires a comprehensive understanding of our resources and defenses." He paused, letting the weight of his words settle. "The tour Tiffany and the boys gave you earlier was just a glimpse. If you're willing to protect what you know, then you need to understand the full extent of what we have, what we need to protect."

After taking them back to the work shed, he led them down the concrete stairs, the air growing cooler with each step. The apartment bunker was the first stop, a stark contrast to the guest rooms in the garage. Each apartment, fully furnished and stocked, was a haven of self-sufficiency. "Parker, Jill," David said, gesturing to one of the apartments. "This is yours. Three bedrooms, a kitchenette, everything you need."

He pointed at the next apartment. "Eric, Bonnie, this one's for you." He smiled at Bonnie. "Plenty of room for you and your toys." Bonnie, wide-eyed, clutched her father's hand. Eric managed a small smile, relief washing over his features.

"Scott, Andrea, Mike," David continued, leading them to their assigned apartment. "Make yourselves at home." Mike, oblivious to the gravity of the situation, was already peering into the kitchenette. "Ooh, snacks!" he exclaimed, grabbing a package of cookies. Andrea sighed, but a grateful smile touched her lips. "These apartments are yours," David emphasized. "Your space, your privacy. But remember, we're a community. We look out for each other."

"Kyle lives down here too, along with my son-in-law's mother," he sighed. "She's at the very bottom, at the very end. If she gives you any trouble, just put her in her place. She's annoying, but harmless." David gestured to the pallets in the hallway. These pallets contain emergency food. Some 'ready to eat', most of it freeze dried. Parker and Eric, you remember delivering this, right?"

He continued the tour, walking them to the house. "Our property has two wells, one at 800 feet, the other at 2,000 feet. This location is unique in that it's more than abundant in that resource." Stopping at the barn, he stomped. "Inside the barn is a maintenance hatch that leads to the propane bunker. Four hundred thousand gallons of liquid propane in eight massive tanks are buried under fifteen feet of earth and concrete, directly below us."

He continued walking. "We also have petroleum and water reserves." As he continued to the house, Scott piped up. "David, doesn't gas have a finite shelf life?" David smiled. "It does, this fuel has been stabilized, and at great cost. We have enough gasoline to last as long as it will hold out. So, about three years. That's why most of what we have runs on propane."

Back in the garage, after revealing the hidden entry way, he guided them deeper into the earth, the air growing colder and more metallic. The storage bunker was a cathedral of supplies, row upon row of food, medicine, and equipment stretching into the dimness. "This," David said, his voice echoing in the vast space, "is our lifeline. Enough food to last for decades, enough medicine to treat any ailment, enough tools to rebuild the world."

Parker, a veteran of countless deployments, was visibly impressed. "This is... incredible," he murmured, shaking his head in disbelief. "I've never seen anything like it." They continued their descent, passing through the recreational bunker with its sparkling pool and running track. Mike was particularly captivated, his eyes gleaming with excitement. "Can we swim, Dad? Can we swim?" he pleaded. "Soon, Mike," Scott said, ruffling his son's hair. "Soon."

Finally, they reached the maintenance bunker, the heart of the entire operation. The air was unusually refreshing, with a faint earthy smell, the quiet hum of the generators a constant undercurrent. David pointed to the massive water silos, the complex hydroponics garden, the greenhouse, the rows of generators humming in perfect synchronization. "This is what keeps us alive," he explained. "The generators provide power, the water silos keep the temperature regulated, the hydroponics garden provides fresh vegetables. Everything is interconnected, everything is essential."

Jill, a practical woman, stepped forward, her eyes narrowed in concentration. "How often do you need to maintain the generators?" she asked. "And what about the hydroponics? I have a green thumb; I could help with that." David smiled, pleased by her initiative. "Excellent question, Jill. Aidan and Alissa handle most of the maintenance, but extra hands are always welcome. And the hydroponics? Jennifer and Brian would be thrilled to have your help."

He looked at the group, their faces a mixture of awe, apprehension, and a newfound sense of purpose. "This is our home now," he said. "And we will defend it together." As they walked back to the apartment bunker, David noticed Bonnie lagging behind, her eyes wide with a mixture of fear and fascination. He knelt beside her, his tone gentle. "Are you okay, Bonnie?" he asked. Bonnie nodded slowly. "It's... a lot," she whispered. "Is it safe here?"

David placed a hand on her shoulder, his gaze unwavering. "It's the safest place in the world, Bonnie. I promise you. We'll protect you." He stood up and offered her his hand. "This bunker, every bunker is two feet of high strength-reinforced concrete. Buried under tons of Texas clay and dirt. The filtration system is so expansive, we will never run out of fresh air. And every system is redundant, even the safety systems."

Back in their apartment, Parker and Jill began unpacking their meager belongings. The apartment was more luxurious than anything they'd ever known, and a sense of hope began to blossom in their hearts. "Do you think we can really make this work?" Jill asked, her voice hesitant. Parker wrapped his arms around her, holding her close. "I don't know," he admitted. "But David has always managed to surprise me."

Meanwhile, in their own apartment, Eric was trying to explain the situation to Bonnie, who managed to find the live feeds of the ranch. "This is our new home, sweetheart," he said. "We're going to be safe here." Bonnie looked up, her eyes still uncertain. "But what about the bad people?" Eric sighed. "David and his family will protect us from the bad people," he said. "They're very strong, and they know what they're doing." He smiled at her, trying to reassure her. "And besides," he added, "we're a part of that family now."

Back in the main house, David sat with his wives in the living room, discussing the day's events. "They're good people," Tiffany said, nodding approvingly. "They'll be a valuable asset to our community." "I agree," Jennifer added. "Especially Jill. She's very observant and has a knack for gardening." David paused a moment. "You remember when I said we needed allies? Well, this is when we collect on that. There will probably be others, which is why I built the apartments."

"First, let them settle in. A few days to decompress. Then, we integrate." He looked at each of his wives in turn, assigning roles with practiced efficiency. "Jennifer, you're up first. Show Jill the greenhouse and hydroponics setup. Explain the system, the crops, the schedule. Jill seems to be quite the gardener, but she needs to adapt to our indoor farming system."

Jennifer grinned, cracking her knuckles. "Consider it done, Master. I'll have her knee-deep in compost by the end of the week." Summer nodded. "Andrea is a nurse. That's incredibly valuable. I'll show her our medical supplies, help her set up a proper aid station. We've got enough medical equipment to rival a small hospital, but it needs to be organized."

David turned to Kayla. "Kayla, you and Jessica give them the grand tour. Laundry, pantry, communal areas. The works. Make sure they know where everything is. And maybe whip up a few welcome cocktails. Nothing too strong. We don't want any accidental security breaches caused by tipsy new arrivals." Kayla chuckled. "On it. Though I reserve the right to judge their taste in spirits."

"David and Kyle will assess their tactical skills. Then they can customize their weapons to their unique style. Make sure they're comfortable and proficient with our standard loadout. And remind him to be patient. Not everyone has spent the last few years prepping for doomsday." "Got it," Kayla responded, already mentally relaying the information to her brother.

David then looked at his children, who were listening intently. "Grace, you keep Bonnie company. Seth, look after Mike. Keep them occupied, answer their questions, make them feel welcome. And keep an eye on them. You both have a knack for noticing things, so if they start feeling overwhelmed or if something's wrong, I want to know." Grace and Seth nodded seriously, taking their responsibilities to heart.

"Tiffany, Nicole, round out the briefing. Focus on ranch operations. Animal care, feeding schedules, maintenance. They need to understand the ecosystem we've built here." Tiffany smiled warmly. "We'll get them up to speed. It's rewarding work, even when there's nothing to do." Nicole added, "It's also a good way to stay grounded. Literally."

He paused, his gaze sweeping over his family. "Finally," he continued, his expression hardening, "remember our rules. Security is paramount. Trust is earned, not given. And loyalty is everything. These people are our guests, but they are also potential liabilities. We need to assess them, train them, and integrate them. Quickly."

Chapter 8

Tanya's Strike Team

"Okay, let's run through it one more time," David stated, his voice clipped but not unkind. "Summer, you've charted the safest route to the medical supply store south of Austin?" Summer consulted the tablet in her hands. "Yes. Minimal highway, mostly backroads. Little David flagged the areas with the most abandoned vehicles on the map, so we can avoid those bottlenecks. Also, the network is still active in the south, so we can use it to monitor for potential threats."

Little David folded his arms. "We'll travel in a staggered formation. Aidan in the lead, Scott bringing up the rear. I'll be in the middle with Summer. Weapons hot." Aidan, finally tearing his attention away from the multi-tool, grinned. "The beast is ready, hard and fast enough to blow your clothes off, but gentle enough to ask for consent."

Scott, a burly man with a construction worker's build, cleared his throat. "I've already reinforced the bed of my truck. We can haul a decent amount of equipment. And Andrea's put together a list of priorities, right?" Andrea nodded, handing David a carefully typed document. "Yes. We're focusing on surgical tools, antibiotics, sutures, IV fluids…the essentials for setting up a proper aid station. We can't rely on finding easily accessible pharmacies in this new reality."

David scanned the list, his mind already calculating the space needed. "Excellent. Use my debit card. Keep receipts. We're still playing by the old rules for now." He paused, a flicker of something akin to amusement in his eyes. "And Summer, try not to buy out the entire store. Remember, we want to avoid escalating any situations. Politeness and legal tender first, firepower as a last resort." Summer chuckled, a mischievous reflection in her eyes. "No promises, David. But I'll try to resist the urge to 'pharmaceutically liberate' everything in sight."

At the conclusion of the meeting, David stood, excusing himself for a… date with Lily? Scott watched with confusion as David left. Meanwhile, his son, David junior took is wife Andrea to the shooting range. "Alright Andrea," Little David said, adjusting the Glock 19 in her hands. "Feet shoulder-width apart, slight bend in the knees. Two-handed grip, thumbs pointing forward. Sight alignment, sight picture. Breathe…squeeze…" He spoke with the crisp authority of a seasoned instructor, a stark contrast to his youthful features. Andrea, a nurse accustomed to sterile environments and precise procedures, absorbed his words with focused intensity. A few rounds in, she was getting the hang of it, her shots weren't in the center of the target, but it was a good start. Little David offered a rare smile. "Good. Consistent. Now, practice drawing from a concealed position. Speed is key, but accuracy is paramount."

Back inside, Scott watched David head down the stairs. "Date with Lily?" he muttered to himself, puzzled. He knew David was devoted to all his wives and children, but he hadn't pegged him as the type for dedicated "date nights" with his nineteen-year-old daughter. Shrugging, he returned to helping Aidan load the trucks, the weight of the mission pressing down on them all.

Later, curiosity gnawing at him, Scott found himself drawn to the recreational bunker. The muffled sounds of rhythmic clanging echoed from within. He descended the stairs cautiously, the low hum of the climate control system filling the air. As he rounded the corner, his jaw dropped.

The sight before him was both mesmerizing and unnerving. David and Lily were engaged in a full-fledged sword fight, their movements a blur of steel and calculated aggression. They were both decked out in body armor, padded in the chest and limbs. Lily, despite her small frame, moved with surprising agility, her platinum hair flying as she parried David's attacks. He, in turn, was a whirlwind of controlled power, his movements fluid and precise, each strike a lesson in both offense and defense.

The air crackled with the clash of steel, the rhythmic grunts of exertion, and the occasional barked instruction from David. "Remember your footwork, Lily! Maintain your balance! Anticipate your opponent's move!" Scott watched, mesmerized, as Lily executed a perfect riposte, forcing David to retreat a step. Her face was alight with focus and determination. This wasn't just father-daughter time; this was serious training, a brutal ballet danced on the edge of survival.

He understood then. This wasn't about dates or father-daughter bonding in the conventional sense. This was about preparing Lily, about instilling in her the skills and mindset she would need to survive in the harsh new world they were facing. A strange mixture of awe and fear washed over him. Awe at the dedication and skill on display, fear at the implications of what it all meant. This was a world where children needed to know how to wield a sword, where quality time involved dodging steel blades and calculating angles of attack.

As the practice continued, Scott noticed the little details. David wasn't just teaching Lily how to fight; he was teaching her how to think, how to adapt, how to survive. He was constantly adjusting his tactics, probing her weaknesses, forcing her to learn and grow. "Good, Lily, but you telegraphed that move," David said, his voice surprisingly gentle despite the intensity of the training. "Keep your movements concealed, your intentions hidden. Surprise is your greatest weapon." Lily nodded, her eyes fixed on her father's. "Yes, Daddy."

David lowered his practice sword, the clang of steel on the padded floor of the recreational bunker echoing. Lily, panting but beaming, mirrored his movement. He adjusted her body armor, his touch surprisingly gentle. "Good work, Lily-bug. You're getting faster. Remember what I said about telegraphing your moves. A flicker of the eyes, a slight shift in your weight – all can betray your intent."

Lily beamed, bouncing on her toes. "I know, Daddy! I'm working on it! Can we do the disarming drill next time?" "We'll see. Now, go get some water. You earned it." He watched her scamper off, a proud smile tugging at his lips. It wasn't exactly playing tea party, but these were the times, and this was how he showed his love. He was preparing her, arming her not just with skill, but with confidence.

Scott, still digesting the spectacle he'd just witnessed, approached David. "That… that was something else, David." David, ever observant, noticed the unease in Scott's voice. "Effective, isn't it? Lily has a natural aptitude for strategy. More than I did, at her age, I didn't start training until I was much older." He paused, a flicker of the old world sadness crossing his face before being quickly masked. "Besides, keeps her off the streets." The attempt at humor fell a little flat, given the situation.

Scott chuckled nervously. "Yeah, well, I guess… streets aren't really a thing anymore." He hesitated, then blurted out, "She really seemed to be enjoying herself." David's smile returned, genuine this time. "She does. It's a challenge, something to focus on. And honestly? She's damn good at it. Better than Tiffany ever was." He winked, then clapped Scott on the shoulder. "Come on, let's get some coffee. Tiffany made a fresh batch. Needs work, but it's coffee."

As they walked towards the stairs that led back up to the main house, Scott couldn't shake the image of Lily, small but fierce, wielding a sword with deadly precision. He thought of his own life before the blackout. After he got out of the Army, he tried to put that life behind him. Now, the reality was survival, and this family was taking it seriously.

Later, Scott headed back to the Apartment bunker, the image of Lily's focused intensity still burned in his mind. As he neared the entryway, he saw Kyle, awkwardly flailing his arms as he faced off against Seth. Seth, not even fifteen, moved with a fluid grace that belied his age, effortlessly deflecting Kyle's wild swings. He wasn't just blocking, he was guiding, correcting, a miniature, albeit rather brutal, sensei. "No, Kyle, you're leading with your shoulder! It's a tell!" Seth patiently explained, disarming Kyle with a swiftness that left him stumbling. "Keep your weight balanced. Think of it like you're rooted to the ground."

Kyle, red-faced and frustrated, wiped his brow. "Easier said than done, kid." "Practice," Seth said simply, then launched into another flurry of calculated strikes, each move designed to expose Kyle's weaknesses. "Again." Scott watched, fascinated and slightly unnerved. He remembered Kyle boasting about his high school wrestling days, but Seth was dismantling him with an almost casual ease, providing constructive criticism throughout.

Scott remembered that day at the waterpark, he remembered Brian and little David. He had to look at the two boys twice to believe it. How could two young boys, barely out of training pants, drag a 250 pound picnic table?

He walked inside the apartment bunker and headed to his apartment. Seeing Parker and Lynn in the hallway. "Hey guys," Scott announced. "Hey Scott, how are you?" Parker asked. "Good, I'm getting settled in, how about you and Jill?" Scott replied. "We're doing well, still learning, but getting the hang of it," Parker responded. "That's good to hear!" Scott said.

Lynn interrupted, "What have you been up to Scott?" "Oh, I was just spending time with Lily and David," Scott answered. "Oh really, how was that?" Lynn asked. "It was good, they were having some father daughter bonding time," Scott replied.

Lynn began to complain, "I don't think David ever treated them like children. Even little Lily is just as bad as her father. They all are." Scott did not want to stay around Lynn and listen to her complaining, "Well, I'll see you guys later." As Scott shut his apartment door, he muttered to himself, "What is going on with this family?"

He replayed all the events he had seen today, the incredible sword fighting skills of Lily, Seth's expertise in combat. "This family is built different," he murmured. It wasn't just the training, the skills, it was something deeper, something ingrained. He sensed an unshakeable combination of competence and discipline, a quiet confidence that bordered on…otherworldly. A chill ran down his spine. He looked around his apartment, a sudden desperate need to reassure himself he was still in the real world, a world of reasonable, average people.

But he wasn't average anymore, was he? He was here, in this valley with this extraordinary, almost unnervingly prepared family. And he realized that his old definition of normal was gone, replaced by something new, something undeniably strange, and maybe, just maybe, something necessary for survival.

Scott woke up with a start, disoriented. He'd fallen asleep on the bed, fully clothed. The smell of Andrea's dinner filled the space, a comforting anchor in the disorienting reality of the bunker. "Where's Mike?" he asked, rubbing the sleep from his eyes. Andrea, without turning from the stove, simply pointed to the LCD window. The wall glowed with the simulated light of late afternoon.

It was like the Barn was right outside their door. Mike was playing tag with Seth amongst the miniature cows. They genuinely looked like they were having a blast, like young teenage boys should. Mike, usually sullen and withdrawn since the blackout, was actually laughing. Seth, despite his preternatural skills and knowledge, seemed to enjoy the simple game just as much.

Then he saw Bonnie, Eric's little girl, and Grace, David and Nicole's daughter. Grace held a makeshift rope leash, and Bonnie sat astride a miniature cow, her face alight with pure joy as Grace led the animal in a slow, wobbly circle. The cow, seemingly unfazed by its tiny rider, chewed placidly on some hay. Meanwhile, the three dachshunds, Homer, Rahab, and Judas, were engaged in a frenzied game of chase, their short legs a blur as they harassed the nonchalant goats. The scene was chaotic, absurd, and strangely... heartwarming.

Scott realized something profound. Even David's children, despite their unsettling abilities and serious demeanor when duty called, knew how to play, how to be kids. And, more importantly, Mike seemed genuinely happy. He watched Mike and Seth high-five after a particularly impressive tag, a genuine smile lighting up Mike's face. For the first time since the world went sideways, Scott felt a flicker of hope. Maybe, just maybe, under David's guidance, in this strange, new world, they could find a way not just to survive, but to live.

He glanced back at Andrea, who was now watching the scene with a soft smile on her face. He walked over and put his arms around her, pulling her close. "Thank you," he whispered. "For what?" she asked, leaning into his embrace. "For being here, for making dinner, for... for everything." She squeezed his hand. "We're in this together, Scott. We always will be."

Andrea kissed her husband before turning back around. "Go tell Mike, dinner's almost done." Scott sighed, looking at the window. He knew that even though he could see his son. Even though he could hear him playing. The reality was that they were twenty feet underground and at least a hundred feet from the front of the barn.

As he started toward the door, Andrea cleared her throat. "Just use the call button," she said, gesturing to the window. Scott furrowed his eyebrows as he returned to the window. There it was, a single round button. Shrugging his shoulders, and feeling slightly embarrassed, he pushed the button. "Mikey. Dinner's almost ready," he said, nervously before turning back to his wife. "Okay dad, I'll be there in a minute," Mike responded.

Scott's eyes widened, he honestly didn't expect a response. In less than a minute, the door opened and there was Mike, smelling of hay and childhood funk. Scott stared at his son, a bemused expression plastered on his face. "How did you hear me so clearly? I practically whispered." Mike shrugged, grabbing a juice box from the counter. "Seth said to listen for the speaker." He popped the straw in and took a long gulp. "David put speakers everywhere." Andrea chuckled. "Apparently, everywhere means wherever there's a camera."

Scott shook his head, still processing the sheer level of detail David incorporated into everything. It was... impressive, if a little overwhelming. He could barely manage to keep the lawn mowed, and here was David, orchestrating a multi-layered bunker system with integrated communication networks and livestock management worthy of a small kingdom. "I'm gonna go wash up," Mike mumbled, heading toward the bathroom.

Scott turned back to Andrea. "This is crazy, right?" "A little," she admitted, stirring a pot on the stove. "But it's our crazy now. And to be honest, I haven't seen Mike this... normal in a long time. So, miniature cow barn speakers and all, I'm grateful."

After dinner, Scott approached the plantation-style house, the setting sun hovering just overhead. He could hear the rhythmic creak of the porch swing and a girl's delighted giggling long before he reached the steps. Scott chuckled, his amusement bubbling over as he approached the porch. There was David, the stoic, paramilitary-trained mastermind behind this entire operation, sporting a ridiculously long-haired wig while his daughter, Lily, meticulously braided it. The contrast was almost too much to bear. "Hey, Scott," David said, his voice perfectly level, completely unfazed by the ridiculousness of the situation. Lily simply giggled and continued her work. "Settling in alright?" Scott struggled to

127

compose himself. "Uh, yeah, settling in. Your place is... something else, David. Seriously. Found the speaker in the barn, by the way. Mike says Seth told him to listen for it."

David nodded, as if finding a hidden speaker system in a miniature cow barn was the most normal thing in the world. "Normalcy is key. Especially during... this." He gestured vaguely towards the darkened landscape beyond the valley. "Plus, I tried to picture myself in that situation. Anything to make this abnormal world seem more... normal." "Right, normalcy," Scott repeated, his lips twitching. He couldn't help but imagine David, in the midst of planning escape routes and rationing supplies, wearing a wig and pausing to install high-fidelity speakers in the barn. "So, what exactly are the cows listening to?" "Classical music," Lily piped up. "It makes the milk taste better."

Scott blinked. Classical music for cows. Of course. "Well, can't argue with that." He shifted uncomfortably. "Look, I wanted to thank you, David. For everything. The apartment, the food, the... cow concerts. It means a lot." David's gaze softened, his eyes crinkling at the corners. "You're welcome, Scott. We're all in this together. Family helps family." He said. Scott nodded, his gaze softening as he thought of his wife and the relief he felt at knowing she was safe and had a purpose. He'd been in a tailspin since the blackout, feeling helpless and useless. Here, with David, he felt like maybe they had a chance.

"So," Scott began, trying to steer the conversation away from his existential crisis, "the wig? Is that part of some... elaborate training exercise?" He gestured towards the ridiculous cascade of synthetic hair. David's lips twitched. "Lily wanted to practice her braiding. So I figured, why not?" "But...the hair?" Lily, the perpetrator of this hairy situation, spoke up, "Daddy's head is too… aerodynamic." Scott burst out laughing, unable to contain it any longer. David, the master strategist, outmaneuvered by a teenager with a penchant for braids.

David didn't seem offended. In fact, a small smile played on his lips. "Sometimes," he said, his voice almost a whisper, "spending time with family isn't always about tactics or training. It's just about… being there." That hit Scott hard. He thought about Mike, about the fear he'd seen in his son's eyes since the world went dark. He'd been so focused on survival, on finding a safe place, that he'd forgotten the most important thing: just being a dad.

He looked at David, at the gentle way he held Lily's hand, at the patience in his eyes as she tugged on the ridiculous wig, the soft criticism as she parried him with a sword. He saw not just a leader, a strategist, or a paramilitary expert, but a father. A real father. "I think I get it," Scott said, his voice quiet. "So, uh, what kind of braids are we talking about here? French? Dutch? Maybe a fishtail?" Lily beamed. "A fishtail! Daddy looks good in fishtails." David sighed dramatically, but there was a hint of amusement in his eyes. "You know Scott, you know an awful lot about braids for a man without daughters."

Scott watched, still processing the wig situation, as Jessica and Tanya walked out onto the porch. Both sat down, sandwiching David between them, each offering a gentle, but affectionate kiss. "Evening, Scott," Jessica greeted with a warm smile. "Settling in okay? Don't mind Lily's... styling choices for Daddy. He's a good sport." A hint of playful sarcasm laced her tone, but her eyes held genuine concern.

Tanya offered Scott a gentle nod. "Welcome to the family, Scott. Anything we can do to help you get comfortable, just let us know." As if on cue, Brian and Seo-Yeon emerged from the house, hand in hand, radiating youthful optimism. Seo-Yeon's genuine smile was infectious.

David observed the scene with a quiet satisfaction, his expression softening as he looked at his family. He then turned to Scott, a spark of an idea in his eyes. "Scott, I have a proposition that may help you all." He leaned in conspiratorially. "Tanya, would you mind taking Taylor, Nicole, and Seo-Yeon and heading to Scott, Parker, and Eric's apartments? I think everyone could use a massage to help them unwind." He paused, his gaze sweeping over the group. "This will also be good practice for Taylor and Nicole," he added with a subtle nod.

Tanya raised an eyebrow. "A massage train? That's... ambitious, even for you, David." But she was already calculating the logistics, her professional instincts kicking in. Seo-Yeon beamed, clearly excited by the idea. David's lips quirked. "Ambitious? Perhaps. Necessary? Absolutely. We need to foster a sense of community, a sense of normalcy. And who doesn't like a good massage?"

Scott blinked, the image of Tanya, Seo-Yeon, Nicole and Taylor descending upon the apartment bunker like a team of tactical relaxation commandos, was certainly novel.

"Massage train?" he repeated, a bewildered smile spreading across his face. "I... I don't know what to say." Jessica chuckled. "Don't worry, Scott. Daddy dearest can be a bit... much sometimes. But he usually has a point. Besides, It's obvious you have all been through a lot. And honestly, when was the last time you had a massage?"

Tanya nodded in agreement. "Exactly. Consider it a welcome gift, Scott. And an opportunity for Taylor and Nicole to hone their skills. Besides, Seo-Yeon's massages are heavenly," she said with a wink. Brian, always eager to help, and fiercely protective of his new wife, chimed in. "I can help you guys carry the massage tables and oils. Anything else you need, just ask."

With a flurry of activity, the massage train began to assemble. Tanya gathered her supplies, Taylor and Nicole, looking slightly nervous but determined, trailed behind her. Seo-Yeon, her smile unwavering, offered Scott a reassuring pat on the arm before joining the procession towards the bunker entrance.

Scott pulled out his phone. "David's sending a deep tissue strike team to the apartments! Tell Jill, Parker and Eric. And judging from the loadout, I don't think the children will be spared either." Andrea, reading Scott's frantic text, nearly choked on her lukewarm coffee. "A deep tissue... strike team?" Her eyes widened. She pictured Tanya, all sleek efficiency, leading a brigade of masseuses armed with scented oils and a mission to knead every stressed muscle into submission. The absurdity of it all struck her, and she burst out laughing.

"What's so funny?" Jill asked, looking up from her book. Parker was meticulously folding his clothes. Eric, Bonnie clinging to his leg, looked warily at Andrea. "Scott says... David's sending a 'deep tissue strike team' to the apartments," Andrea managed, gasping between fits of laughter. "Apparently, it's a 'massage train' intended to relieve stress. The children are not spared."

Jill's eyebrows shot up. "A massage train? That's... certainly one way to maintain morale during the end times." She exchanged a glance with Parker, who had stopped folding his laundry, a flicker of amusement in his eyes. Eric, however, looked genuinely terrified. "A massage train? Is this some kind of... weird torture thing David does? I signed up for safety, not... forced relaxation!" Bonnie, sensing his anxiety, tightened her grip on his leg.

Andrea, still chuckling, tried to reassure him. "Eric, relax. It's just a massage. Tanya's a professional, and I heard Seo-Yeon's amazing. Besides, it's not like you can refuse. David is... persuasive, remember?" She shuddered slightly, remembering the unwavering, yet gentle, look David had given her earlier that morning. Parker, ever the stoic veteran, spoke up. "Look, even if it's a little... unorthodox, a massage probably wouldn't hurt anyone. We're all carrying a lot of tension. Just... try to relax. And if they start using hot stones or anything, someone scream."

As the "deep tissue strike team," led by Tanya, entered the apartment bunker, they were met with a mixture of apprehension and curiosity. Scott, standing awkwardly by the entrance to his apartment, attempted a weak smile. Andrea, attempting to stifle another giggle, steered Eric and a wide-eyed Bonnie towards their own unit. Parker, ever observant, simply nodded a greeting, his inner turmoil masked by a stoic facade. Jill gave David's wives a warm smile, she had always been a sucker for a good massage.

Chapter 9

The Extraction Team

David, perched on a stool at the counter, sipped his coffee, his gaze flitting between Jessica and the meticulous checklist in his hand. He ran the calculations in his head one more time: fuel consumption, estimated travel time, potential threats, contingencies A through Z. "David, honey," Summer called from the hallway. "Little David says the route's been uploaded to Aidan's GPS and Scott's tablet. He also triple-checked the tire pressure on all the vehicles." "Excellent," David said, marking the items off his list with a satisfying click of his pen. Little David was proving to be an invaluable asset.

Meanwhile, in the garage, Aidan revved the engine of his red beast. While a radio crackled on the workbench, relaying updates from David inside. Scott nervously adjusted the straps of his tactical vest. Andrea, already geared up, gave his shoulder a reassuring squeeze. "We've got this, Scott. Just stick to the plan." Mike, clung to Andrea's leg, wide-eyed.

David finally stepped into the garage, his presence instantly commanding attention. "Alright, people," he announced. "Let's keep this simple. Aidan, remember, you're point. Little David, you're riding with Summer. Scott, you bring up the rear. Stay alert, stay focused, and stick to the route. Any questions?"

Lynn hovered near the entrance of the garage. Her eyes darted nervously between David and her son, Josh, who was busy helping Aidan load extra propane into the Red Beast. "Yes, I have a question," Lynn interrupted, her voice trembling. "Will Josh be safe?" David fixed her with a stare that could freeze magma. "Josh is family. His safety is my priority, along with everyone here." The emphasis was clear: don't question his decisions. Lynn shrunk back, muttering something about just being a concerned mother.

He turned his attention back to the convoy. "All vehicles, this is Romeo-one, radio check," David commanded. Aidan's voice crackled over the radio. "Red Beast, read you lima charlie." Summer's voice followed. "Whiskey-three, loud and clear." "Sierra Yankee, read you loud and clear," Scott replied, his voice slightly shaky. "Excellent. Move out." The Red Beast roared to life, leading the way out of the garage and onto the long, winding driveway. Summer's vehicle followed, Little David sitting beside her, his face impassive as he scanned the surrounding hillside. Scott's truck brought up the rear, Andrea gripping the dashboard, her knuckles white.

Back inside the house, David and Brian settled into the command center, a converted living room with several radios, maps, and a tablet, monitoring their location. "Anything on the airwaves?" David asked, his eyes glued to a map of the planned route. "Just the usual static and some chatter about looters near Waco," Brian reported. "Nothing that should interfere with the convoy." David nodded, a muscle twitching in his jaw. He trusted Little David's route planning, but in this new world, trust was a luxury he couldn't afford.

Nearly an hour later, David was still monitoring the convoy's progress, Tiffany, Jennifer and Lynn watching quietly. "They should be there shortly. So far, so good," David said, not looking up. Jessica remained perched behind him, her head resting on his back. "I hope they make it back soon," she mumbled, squeezing him tightly.

The journey to Austin proved to be rather uneventful. Andrea, with her list, was quick to pick out everything she needed, her husband following close behind her. As Scott loaded the back of his truck, Josh kept a watchful eye. Meanwhile, Summer was on the other side of the warehouse, loading up on pharmaceuticals. Then the power suddenly went out, plunging Summer into near darkness. Dust motes danced in the faint light filtering through the grimy windows. A chill snaked down her spine, a primal fear she hadn't felt since... well, since the world went sideways ten days ago.

Her hand instinctively went to the pistol holstered at her hip. She was no stranger to firearms, thanks to David's... thorough... preparations. The memory of hours spent at the range, under David's meticulous instruction, was a comfort, a tangible reminder of his unwavering dedication to their safety. "Damn it," she muttered, her voice echoing slightly in the sudden silence. She pulled out her flashlight, its beam cutting through the gloom. She quickly located the pre-packed bags she'd been filling with antibiotics, antiseptics, and pain relievers. David had drilled into them the importance of speed and efficiency in dangerous situations. Panic was a luxury they couldn't afford.

She grabbed the bags and headed for the front of the warehouse, her senses on high alert. Every creak of the building, every rustle from the loading dock sent a jolt of adrenaline through her. She rounded a corner and nearly collided with a shadow lurking near the entrance. "Easy," a voice said, and Summer lowered her flashlight, recognizing Aidan's familiar silhouette. He held his AR-15 at the ready, his young face etched with concern. "Power went out. We're securing the perimeter." "I think it's out for good," Summer replied, trying to keep her voice steady. "I've got the supplies. Let's get out of here."

Outside, the midday sun seemed almost blinding after the dimness of the warehouse. Josh and Scott were scanning the surroundings, their faces grim. Little David stood perched on the hood of the truck, his eyes narrowed, a sniper rifle resting across his lap. Even at his young age, his focus was unnervingly sharp, a testament to the skills David had instilled in him. "What happened?" Scott asked, his hand hovering near his own weapon. "Power outage," Aidan explained. " Summer got the supplies, let's move."

They loaded the bags quickly and efficiently, a well-oiled machine forged in the crucible of the apocalypse. Everybody loaded up, and they peeled out of the parking lot, leaving the silent, darkened warehouse behind. As they drove, Summer couldn't shake the unease that had settled over her. It wasn't just the blackout; it was a feeling, a premonition that something was about to change. The relative calm they had experienced in the last ten days felt like a fragile bubble about to burst.

Some time later, as David monitored the progress of the convoy, the jarring screech of metal on asphalt ripped through the radio static, followed by Summer's strained voice. "Spike strip... we're hit! We're disabled, off the road." David's jaw tightened. The radio crackled again, this time Scott's voice, laced with frustration. "Truck's drivable, but we've got four flats. Looks like a professional job." "Location?" David barked into the radio, his mind already calculating the best course of action. He glanced at the faces of his wives, each one a mirror of his own concern, their training kicking in. "About five miles north of the bridge on I-35," Scott replied, his voice shaky. "Looks like we're sitting ducks here."

"Understood. Standby. We're mobilizing a recovery team." David turned to his wives, his voice calm despite the icy knot forming in his stomach. "Elena, get Brian and Lily. We need a full extraction team geared up and ready to roll in five minutes. Tanya, medical kit, trauma supplies, in the van. Jessica, stay here and monitor the radio."

Elena moved quickly, years of drills and contingency planning etched into her muscle memory. Tanya, still new to the situation, ran downstairs and loaded the triage kit into the van. Jessica, despite being over a month pregnant, remained a pillar of calm, her fingers already dancing across the radio console. David strode towards the armory, his mind already racing through potential threats.

He entered the armory, the familiar scent of gun oil and steel a strange comfort. He quickly grabbed his Beretta, his wakizashi, and his 338 Lapua Magnum, checking each one with meticulous precision. He grabbed several magazines, a tactical vest, and a thermal imaging scope.

Lily and Brian, already clad in tactical gear, were waiting for him as he exited the armory. Seth, and Grace stood behind them, weapons at the low ready, their young faces grimly determined. "Dad, we're ready," Brian said, his voice firm, his eyes mirroring David's own resolve. "Brian, you're on overwatch. Lily, you're the gunner. Seth, maintain radio contact. And Grace, prep the trauma kit." David issued the orders with crisp authority, as his children silently nodded.

They piled into the Ford Transit, its engine roaring to life. David took the wheel, his hands firm on the controls. Brian sat beside him, scanning the road ahead. Lily settled into the gunner's seat on the roof, David's rifle at the ready. Seth and Grace sat in the back, their weapons trained on the side roads. As they sped down the highway, David felt a surge of grim determination. He couldn't afford to lose anyone. He had a responsibility to protect his family, to guide them through this chaos.

"Report," David commanded, his voice cutting through the roar of the engine. "No visual contact, but I'm picking up signs of recent activity," Lily reported from the roof, her voice calm and professional. "Looks like they cleared out fast." "Seth, any radio chatter?" David asked. "Negative, Dad," he replied.

They rounded a bend in the road and came upon the scene. Summer's car lay in a ditch, its tires shredded. Scott's truck sat a short distance away, its tires deflated. Aidan and

Josh were on the near end, scanning the wood line. Andrea and Scott were behind their truck, hiding behind the axles. "All clear!" Lily yelled. "Let's go!"

The van screeched to a halt, and the extraction team sprang into action. Lily provided overwatch from the roof, while Brian, joined by Aidan and Josh, fanned out, securing the perimeter. David approached Summer's car, he could see the relief wash over her face as she saw him approach. "Are you hurt?" he asked, his voice filled with concern. "Just shaken up," Summer replied, her voice trembling slightly. "That came out of nowhere. Professional, efficient. They knew what they were doing."

David examined the spike strip. It was meticulously placed, almost invisible against the asphalt. "They were waiting for you," he said grimly. "We need to get out of here. Now." "What about the vehicles?" Scott asked, his voice filled with frustration. "Load everything into the van," David replied. "Right now, our priority is getting everyone back to the ranch. Andrea, how are you doing?" "I'm fine, just a few scratches," Andrea replied, relief evident on her face.

David quickly assessed the situation. They couldn't risk staying here any longer. The attackers could return at any moment. "Load everything into the van. Aidan, you're with me. Summer, once they're done, take the van back to the ranch," David ordered. As Lily continued to scan the area, Scott, Andrea and Summer loaded the medical supplies into the back of the van. Meanwhile, little David, Aidan, Josh and Lily continued to provide cover. Suddenly, a shot was fired. David turned quickly to see Lily charging the bolt as she reloaded his rifle. "Daddy! The thermal imaging is picking up bodies in the trees, at least seven, possibly six, now!"

Aidan and little David ducked behind the truck as David signaled for Summer to go. After Summer, Josh, Andrea and Scott boarded, the van took off, disappearing down the road. However, in the oncoming lane, two vehicles, one truck and one SUV, hidden in plain sight, turned around and began following them. "Seth, you've got two coming up from the rear, one pickup and one dark SUV," David said, turning his attention back to the tree line.

The air crackled with gunfire. David, his senses hyper-alert, dropped to a low crouch behind the truck. Aidan and Little David mirrored his movements, their faces grim and focused. "Positions, angles, communicate," David barked, his voice barely audible above the din. Aidan, nimble and quick, scrambled to the opposite side of the truck, using the engine block as cover. Little David crawled under the vehicle, seeking a lower vantage point. "Contact right, two in the pines, suppressed," Aidan reported, squeezing off two precise shots that chipped bark from the trees. "Contact left, three behind the sedan, one moving to flank," Little David's voice crackled from beneath the truck. He punctuated his report with a burst of semi-automatic fire, forcing the flanking attacker to scramble for cover.

David, scanning the space in between, spotted the sixth assailant – a figure partially concealed behind a cluster of rocks, attempting to get a clear shot at Aidan. With a careful hand, he raised his pistol, steadied his aim, and squeezed the trigger. The figure slumped to the ground. "One

141

down, rocks," David announced, scanning the area. "Aidan, pressure the pines. Junior, watch for the flanker. I'll cover the sedan."

The firefight intensified. Bullets whizzed past, chewing up metal. The acrid smell of gunpowder filled the air. David moved with a calculated grace, using the ruined vehicles as cover, suppressing fire and eliminating threats with ruthless efficiency. Aidan, with his father's precision and his own youthful energy, kept the two in the pines pinned down. Little David, seemingly firing from an endless magazine, continued to harass the flanker, preventing them from gaining a strategic advantage.

Minutes stretched into an eternity as the three-man team systematically dismantled the ambush. Finally, after what seemed like an age, the firing ceased. An eerie silence descended upon the scene. "Clear," Aidan announced, cautiously emerging from behind the truck. "Clear," Little David echoed, crawling out from under the vehicle, his face smeared with grime.

David, his gaze sweeping the perimeter, remained cautious. "Stay sharp," he ordered. "They might have reinforcements." He approached the downed assailants, confirming their demise. These weren't just thugs; their equipment was professional, their tactics well-rehearsed. This was more than a random highway robbery. Someone had targeted them. "They're good," Aidan said, examining a fallen enemy's weapon. "Too good for normies." "Agreed," David responded, his voice hard. "This was organized. Take their weapons and ammo, plus anything else worth keeping. Torch the bodies, I don't want anything left."

Meanwhile, miles away on the highway, Summer gripped the steering wheel, her knuckles white. Beside her, Brian monitored the rearview mirrors, his face a mask of concentration. Seth and Grace, in the back, kept their weapons trained on the road behind them. Suddenly, Brian swore under his breath. "Vehicles approaching, fast. Two of them. Matching the description dad gave."

Summer's heart pounded in her chest. "Lily, Status," Summer began, but before she could finish, Lily responded. "Negative on call, Ma," Lily's voice was clear and without hesitation, "I'm prioritizing eliminating threats." And eliminate she did. The first vehicle, a weathered pickup truck, attempted to overtake them. Lily, bracing herself against the roll bar, took aim through her scope. Her first shot shattered the windshield, sending shards of glass flying. Her second shot found its mark, hitting the driver. The truck swerved wildly before crashing into the median.

"One down, another approaching!" Brian shouted, his voice strained. "They're flanking us on the right!" The second vehicle, a black SUV, slowed momentarily before accelerating again, its occupants firing wildly. Lily, unfazed, returned fire. Summer wrestled with the steering wheel, weaving through the abandoned cars that littered the highway. The SUV was relentless, its driver skilled and determined.

Lily, her movements fluid and precise, continued to fire, picking off the remaining attackers one by one. The SUV, riddled with bullets, finally began to falter. Its driver, wounded and desperate, made a last-ditch attempt to ram the van. Lily, anticipating the move, fired a single, well-placed shot that disabled the engine. The SUV sputtered, coughed, and ground to a halt. "Threat neutralized," Lily announced, her voice calm and collected. Summer, breathing heavily, continued toward the ranch.

Back at the ambush site, David, Aidan, and Little David finished burning the bodies, smoke billowing to the sky. "Junior, grab that spike strip and put it in the trunk," Aidan ordered, getting into the driver's seat. As quickly as they arrived, David and his boys were back on the road.

Aidan expertly maneuvered the Red Beast, as he approached the wreckage of the overturned pickup truck. The truck's tires spun uselessly in the air, a grotesque imitation of life. He gestured at the wreck. "Cautious approach. Aidan, secure the perimeter. Junior, cover me." Aidan hopped out, immediately checking the area for others. Little David held his rifle with the steady confidence of a seasoned marksman.

The driver of the pickup was beyond help, twisted at an unnatural angle within the cab, his brains a splattered mess on the back glass. David bypassed him, focusing on the passenger slumped against the dashboard, blood blooming on his chest. He was alive, barely, his eyes fluttering open and closed.

David knelt, pulling out his Wakizashi, the polished steel gleaming in the harsh sunlight. "Why were you following the van." His voice was calm, devoid of emotion. It was a tool, an instrument designed to extract information efficiently. The man groaned, his words slurred and choked

with pain. "Don't... know... just... told to follow..."
"Follow who? Where?" David pressed, the edge of the blade resting lightly against the man's throat, a silent promise.

The man's eyes widened in panic. "The woman... that's all I know! Please..." David's mind raced. The van. Summer, Andrea, Scott, Josh. They were heading back to the ranch, vulnerable. He couldn't risk them being followed. He had to ensure this man revealed everything he knew. But judging by his panicked expression, pain & blurred recollection, he couldn't possibly know more than he claimed.

"You're useless," David stated simply, the words devoid of malice, merely a factual observation. With a swift, almost surgical movement, he separated the man's head from his body. No wasted movements, no unnecessary suffering. Efficiency. Aidan and Little David were already back in the car, engines idling. David wiped the blade clean on the dead man's shirt, took his firearms, and returned to his sons.

A few miles further down the highway, they found the SUV. Its body littered with holes, steam hissing from the ruined engine. The air hung thick with the acrid smell of burnt rubber and gasoline. Inside, three bodies lay still, grotesque puppets tangled in seatbelts. The driver, however, was alive, slumped over the steering wheel, coughing weakly. Again, David approached cautiously, Little David covering him with practiced ease. The driver looked up, his face contorted in pain and fear.

"Who are you?" David asked, his voice a low, dangerous rumble. "Why were you following the van?" The driver spat a mouthful of blood. "We... we just wanted what you had. Supplies. Food. You can't blame us." "Who sent you?" David pressed, his gaze unwavering. The driver hesitated, his eyes darting nervously around the wreckage. "Nobody… we were just… desperate." David didn't believe him. Desperation was a powerful motivator, but this felt… organized. He looked into the man's eyes, reading his true emotions. Fear, uncertainty and hesitation confirmed his suspicions.

He weighed his options. He could interrogate this man for information, but it would be time-consuming, and might not yield any useful results. He also couldn't transport the man. He was too badly injured, and the risk of infection was too high, plus, there was no way he was bringing an outsider to his ranch. Each decision always comes with a sacrifice. "You're lying," David said flatly. He quickly ended the man's life, just like the last. "Aidan, check the bodies for anything of value. Junior, secure the perimeter." He watched as his sons efficiently went about their tasks.

As Aidan searched the bodies, he found a crudely folded piece of paper in one of the dead man's pockets. He handed it to David, who unfolded the paper carefully. It was a hand-drawn map, crudely sketched, but recognizable. It depicted the area around his ranch, with a red circle. Next to the circle, the words. "Possible paramilitary compound, David's Ranch." This was them. Whoever posted the map online, sent them. "We need to tell the others," he said, his voice urgent. "They might be planning another attack. This time, they'll be prepared." Aidan nodded, his face grim. Little

David checked his rifle one last time and got into the Red Beast, his eyes narrowed, scanning the horizon.

As the Red Beast roared into the garage, kicking up dust and gravel. David, Aidan, and Little David piled out, their faces grim. Relief washed over the women as they saw their husbands and sons, but the tension in the air was palpable. "What happened?" Tiffany asked, her voice tight with concern. David, his eyes scanning the perimeter, wasted no time. "They were after Summer. A pickup and an SUV. They had a map of the ranch."

A ripple of unease spread through the group. Elena, ever the strategist, stepped forward. "Did you find out who sent them?" "Not specifically," David replied, his jaw clenched. "But they were definitely targeting us. They knew about the ranch." He held up the crumpled map, its crude markings a familiar image. Summer gasped, her hand flying to her mouth. Jessica, still pale from the day's events, clutched Luci tighter.

"We need to be vigilant," David continued, his voice regaining its authoritative edge. "This wasn't random. Someone is coming for us." He continued as he removed his gear. "Obviously they already know about the ranch, but they haven't come after us directly. Which means, they know how fortified we are. I surmise they went after Summer."

"Honey, is there something… about me?" Summer asked, her voice shaking. He reached out, taking her hand in his. "No, Summer. Absolutely not. You are incredible. You're intelligent, empathetic, and you have a way of seeing the best in everyone." He paused, his gaze hardening. "That's what makes you a target. They think they can use your kindness against me, against us."

Elena scoffed, leaning against the doorframe. "They're underestimating you, Summer. And they're definitely underestimating us." Jennifer playfully slapped at Elena's arm. "Don't go all 'provocateur' on her, Elena. Summer knows we're a team." David nodded, squeezing Summer's hand. "Exactly. They see a soft target, someone they can exploit. It could have been any one of you. Any one of us. They think they can make me crack. But they don't know who they're dealing with."

Jennifer straightened. "Do we need to increase our defenses? More patrols? Maybe reinforce the perimeter even further?" David shook his head, a grim set to his jaw. "No. Overreacting plays into their hands. What happened today was contained. Yes, it was brutal, but in the end, thirteen of them lie dead, and we all walked away. We handled it. Panic is their weapon, and we won't give them the satisfaction." He paused, his gaze sweeping over each of them. "We are prepared. We are strong. We will not be intimidated."

"Everyone is to remain armed at all times, especially outside the house. Travel in pairs, no exceptions. And be aware of your surroundings. Trust your instincts. If something feels off, it probably is." The faces of his older children, Aidan, Brian, little David, and Lily, were stone. They knew exactly what he meant.

He turned his attention to Aidan. "Aidan, begin fortifying the remaining vehicles. Add extra plating, reinforce the windows, upgrade the engines, and I want run-flat inserts in all of our tires." "Already on it, Dad," Aidan replied, his voice steady. "Alissa and I can start tomorrow morning." "Good. And find another truck for Aidan to turn into a 'beast'. Something heavy-duty. Something that can take a beating and keep on going." David knew that, with Aidan's skills, he could turn any truck into monster.

Then, his gaze swept across the room, pausing on each of his wives. "I also want everyone that's not a crack shot on the range 10 hours a day. Anyone struggling to get around in body armor, put them in panels and plates until they can't walk. Get them used to the weight, the restriction. It could save their lives." He paused, his expression softening slightly as he looked at Jessica, her hand resting protectively over her small bump. "We'll adjust the training for you, Jess. Your safety, and the baby's, is paramount."

Finally, he delivered his last pronouncement, his voice leaving no room for argument. "And make sure they know that pool privileges are now earned. Any one that falls short, is confined to the ranch. For their safety and ours. Anyone incapable of pulling their own weight is a liability." Elena, sensing an opportunity to stir the pot, piped up. "So, who's going to tell Lynn she's grounded until further notice?"

Chapter 10

Josh's Manly Moment

"So," Josh began hesitantly, fiddling with the edge of his flannel shirt. He was usually a confident farm boy, but around David, especially when surrounded by David's formidable family, he sometimes felt like a field mouse in a room full of hawks. "I was just wondering something." David, ever attentive, raised an eyebrow. "Wonder away, Josh, that's what we're here for." Josh cleared his throat. "Well, it's about... Lynn. My mom." A ripple of barely suppressed amusement travelled through the women. Tiffany choked back a laugh, while Jennifer simply raised her eyebrows suggestively.

David's smile faltered, but he remained composed. Lynn. Even in this life, she managed to be a source of... mild irritation. In his previous life, she had been his wife for nearly two decades. An experience he wouldn't wish on his worst enemy. "What about her?" he asked carefully. "Well," Josh began, "I know... I know you were married to her before. In your... other life." He stumbled over the words, still slightly incredulous about the whole regression thing. "And I was just wondering... what was she like? Back then?"

David sighed inwardly. He'd known this question was coming eventually. Josh, despite being a good kid, was loyal to his mother, even if Lynn's overbearing nature often drove him crazy. He supposed it was natural for him to try and reconcile the image of the woman he knew with the vague references David had made to their past. "She was... complex," David said diplomatically, taking a sip of his tea. "A good person, at her core. But... perpetually dissatisfied." "Dissatisfied?" Josh frowned. "With what?" "With everything, it seemed," David chuckled mirthlessly. "Nothing was ever quite good enough. And rather than offer trust or encouragement, her default setting was... critical analysis."

Josh scratched Rahab behind the ears, his brow furrowed. "Mom's always been... particular," he admitted. "She worries a lot. But she means well." "I know she does," David assured him. "But back then... it felt like I was constantly falling short. Like I could never quite measure up to her expectations. So eventually... I stopped trying so hard."

He paused, lost in thought for a moment. He remembered the endless cycle of trying to please her, of attempting to bridge the gap between them. He'd tried everything – romantic gestures, practical help, even attempting to engage in her hobbies. But each attempt had been met with suspicion or criticism. "She saw my attempts at connecting as... 'weaponized marital tactics'," David said, the bitterness still lingering after all these years. "Like every kind thing I did had an ulterior motive. Like I was trying to manipulate her."

Josh looked horrified. "Mom thought that? Really?" David nodded. "She always saw me as reckless, uncaring, unloving," he explained. "And the more I tried to prove her wrong, the more she seemed to believe it." He took another

151

sip of his tea, the hot liquid doing little to soothe the harshness of the memories. He remembered the frustration, the loneliness, the feeling of constantly walking on eggshells. "It was... exhausting," he confessed. "And ultimately, unsustainable."

Josh remained silent, absorbing David's words. He knew his mother could be difficult, but hearing it from David, someone who had actually been married to her, painted a stark picture. "Did she... did she at least try to understand you?" Josh asked quietly. David hesitated. "I don't think she was capable of it," he said finally. "She had a preconceived notion of who I was, and she wasn't willing to let go of it, no matter what I did."

He thought back to the last time the blackout had happened. The memory was still vivid, even with the years that separated him from it. He remembered the fear, the uncertainty, and the desperate need to protect his children. "When the world went dark before," David went on, "Greg, Jeremy, and Matthew... my sons... instinctively took on protective roles. They wanted to help, to defend. They understood the dangers of the situation." David paused. "You see, my sons took after me. Even when the courts took them away, it seems she couldn't escape my influence."

"But Mom...?" Josh prompted. "Lynn thought weapons were too dangerous, that they couldn't be trusted with them," David said flatly. "She didn't want them around. So they weren't welcome." He shook his head, a wave of sadness washing over him. "Rather than letting them stay with her at her parents' house, where she felt safe, they stayed in their own apartments. Which, of course, were easy targets." The unspoken implication hung heavy in the air. In the previous timeline, his sons had been vulnerable, exposed, because their own mother had prioritized her fear over their safety.

Josh winced. "That's... that's awful." "It was," David agreed. "And it's a lesson I've carried with me. This time, things are different. This time, my family is prepared. This time, we're not relying on hope and good intentions." He looked at Josh, his eyes filled with a mixture of determination and regret. "Lynn is a good person, Josh. I truly believe that. But she's also... limited. And sometimes, good intentions aren't enough."

He stood up, placing his empty glass on the table. "Don't misunderstand me, Josh," he said, placing a hand on the younger man's shoulder. "I'm not telling you this to make you hate your mother. I'm telling you this, so you understand. So you can make your own choices, based on your judgment, not just on what she tells you."

As the family gathered for dinner, Josh joined Lily at David's table. The aroma of Tanya's Bulgogi filled the air. "This smells really good Miss Tanya," Josh complimented. "You think this is good, you should try David's Bulgogi. He taught me how to make it," Tanya responded as she placed the rice on the table. Josh looked at David, who didn't even look up. "Of course he did," Josh mumbled.

As they ate, Josh sat beside Lily, stealing glances at her. She was recounting the details of their impromptu high-speed chase. As she mimicked the recoil of the rifle, her elbow bumped Josh's shoulder. "And then boom! Clean shot through the engine block! The whole truck just stuttered and died." He swallowed, the bulgogi momentarily losing its savory appeal. Lily, his Lily, was a stone-cold shot. He, on the other hand, had nearly tripped over the running board trying to get into the van.

"Impressive, Lily-bug," David said. "I saw the aftermath of your fine work when we caught up to the vehicles you shut down..." As David spoke, Josh felt a familiar pang of inadequacy. David, the epitome of efficiency and competence, was praising his wife for her skills. He knew David wasn't trying to make him feel bad, but the comparison was unavoidable.

He stabbed at a piece of kimchi with his fork, the spicy tang doing little to alleviate his sour mood. He thought of his mother, Lynn, likely huddled in her apartment bunker, terrified and probably blaming him for not being there to protect her. He'd spent years trying to appease her, anticipating her needs, living his life according to her expectations. David's blunt assessment of Lynn's personality from earlier echoed in his mind.

"Josh, honey, you alright?" Lily nudged him, her brow furrowed with concern. "You seem a million miles away." "Just thinking," he mumbled, avoiding her gaze. "Thinking about what?" She persisted, gently touching his hand. He looked up, meeting her clear blue eyes. He saw genuine affection there, a depth of understanding that he hadn't fully appreciated. "Thinking about... everything. About the chase, about Mom, about..." he trailed off, unable to articulate the complex knot of emotions swirling inside him. Josh continued eating his dinner, however, Lily had grabbed his hand and refused to let go for the duration of the meal.

Later, after dinner, as the younger children were being ushered off to bed, Josh found himself alone with Lily on the back porch. The crickets chirping in the distance. "So," Lily said, leaning against the porch railing, "spill it. What's really going on in that head of yours?" He sighed, running a hand through his hair. "I just... I feel like I'm failing. You're amazing, Lily. You're strong, you're smart, you can shoot the wings off a fly at a hundred yards. And me? I'm just... me."

Lily laughed, a light, airy sound that chased away some of the darkness. "Josh, you're being ridiculous. Of course, you're you! That's why I married you!" "But I'm not like David," he blurted out, the words tumbling out before he could stop them. "I'm not as decisive, as capable..." Lily stepped closer, cupping his face in her hands. "You're not Dad, and that's not a bad thing. Dad is... Dad. He's amazing in his own way, but he's not you. I didn't marry Dad. I married you, Josh. The kind, caring, sometimes goofy guy who makes me laugh and who always knows how to make me feel better when I'm down."

Her words, so simple and honest, hit him with unexpected force. He had been so focused on trying to emulate David, on trying to live up to some impossible standard, that he had completely lost sight of who he was, "and more importantly, who Lily loved. "And about your mom," Lily continued, her expression softening, "you can't keep living your life for her, Josh. I know she's your mother,

155

and you love her, but you need to put yourself first. You're my husband now. You have a responsibility to me, to yourself, to be the best you that you can be."

He finally understood. Lily's desire for him to be more assertive wasn't about becoming a carbon copy of David. It was about him embracing his own strengths, his own potential, and becoming the man she knew he could be. And it certainly wasn't about him being her dad.

Lily leaned close, wrapping her arms around him. "Would it make you feel better if I called you Daddy?" she asked, waggling her eyebrows. Josh stifled a laugh, nearly spitting on her face. As they walked inside, David called out, sitting like a phantom in the living room.

"So," David began, his voice calm and measured, "I see you two had a... productive conversation." He laced his fingers together, his gaze unwavering as he looked at Josh. The young man shifted uncomfortably, his Adam's apple bobbing. "Yeah, well, I... I said some stupid things," Josh mumbled, avoiding eye contact. "I just... I don't know. I feel like I'm not good enough." David nodded slowly. "Good enough for Lily? Good enough for this family? Or good enough for yourself?" Josh swallowed hard. "All of the above, I guess."

David pushed himself up from the armchair. "I understand that feeling, Josh. The feeling of inadequacy. Of constantly measuring yourself against others, especially someone you admire." He paused, his eyes softening slightly, "Believe it or not, I've been there. He walked over to the fireplace, his movements deliberate and purposeful. "I grew up with a father who only saw value in what I could do for him. Could I use a Skil saw? Could I help him fix a car? Could I impress him with my art? Only then was I worthy of his attention. And a mother… well, she only cared if I could cook a decent meal and keep a tidy house. It was exhausting."

A flicker of understanding crossed Josh's face. David continued, "And then there was Lynn," David visibly winced, "She expected me to act exactly how she wanted." He didn't want to go too deep into that, but the point was clear. "It wasn't until I met Samantha, someone who just wanted me to be me, that I realized how warped my perception of value had become," he said, smiling at Jessica.

He turned back to Josh, his expression earnest. "Josh, your value isn't determined by how well you stack up against me or anyone else. Your value is inherent. It's in your kindness, your willingness to help, your unwavering compassion for Lily. It's in your ability to fix things with duct tape and a prayer when everyone else is scrambling for specialized tools. Those are your strengths. Own them."

Lily reached for Josh's hand, squeezing it reassuringly. "See? What did I tell you?" she said softly. David turned his attention to Lily. "Lily, I understand your frustration. You see Josh's potential, and you want him to step into it. But you have to let him do it on his own terms. You chose him for who he is, not who you want him to be." "I know, Dad," Lily sighed, "It's just hard sometimes. Especially with all this…" she gestured vaguely around the room, encompassing the fortified house and the unstable world outside. "…going on. I just want to make sure we're prepared."

"Preparedness isn't about everyone being a carbon copy of me, Lily," David said, his voice firm. "It's about utilizing everyone's unique strengths and working together as a cohesive unit." He looked back at Josh. "You and Lily are a team. Two halves of a whole. You don't need to compete, you need to cooperate."

An idea began to form in David's mind, a practical solution that would not only address the immediate issue but also lay the groundwork for the future. "Speaking of teams," David began, his tone shifting to a more business-like cadence, "I've been thinking about restructuring some of our security details."

Josh and Lily exchanged confused glances. "Security details?" Josh asked. "Yes. With everything that's been going on," David said, referring to the incident from yesterday, "we need to optimize our resources. And I think pairing you two permanently makes perfect sense."

Lily's eyes widened. "You mean... together? Even on patrols?" "Exactly. Lily, you're a natural leader, a skilled marksman, and you have an intuitive understanding of tactics. But you can't be everywhere at once. Josh, you may not have Lily's combat prowess, but your calm demeanor, your resourcefulness, and your ability to de-escalate tense situations are invaluable assets. You complement each other perfectly."

David continued, "Furthermore, Josh, you can take over managing supplies and inventory on security runs. I can't have Lily being distracted by these tasks during missions" David knew that even if Josh wasn't as naturally proficient as

Lily in certain areas, his attention to detail and his willingness to learn would make him a valuable asset. And more importantly, it would give him a sense of purpose and belonging, solidifying his place within the family structure. It was about finding a role where he could contribute meaningfully, where his strengths could shine.

"So," David concluded, a hint of a smile playing on his lips, "what do you say? Ready to be a permanent security team?" Josh looked at Lily, a newfound sense of confidence in his eyes. "Yeah," he said, his voice firm. "Yeah, I'm ready." Lily grinned, squeezing his hand again. "Me too." David nodded, satisfied. "Good. Then consider it done." He paused. "And Josh, one more thing. Lay off the self-deprecating humor, alright? It's getting old." Josh chuckled, a genuine, unforced sound. "Will do, David."

Later that night, the gentle splashing of water echoed from the adjoining bathroom. Lily had drawn herself a bath, the scent of lavender drifting into the bedroom where Josh sat on the edge of the bed, replaying the day's events. The weight of responsibility, the thrill of David's approval, and the burgeoning feelings he had for Lily swirled inside him, a heady cocktail of emotions. He rose, intending to grab a towel from the bathroom, his mind still preoccupied. He pushed the door open without knocking, expecting to find an empty room. He was wrong.

The room was filled with fragrant steam. Lily was in the bathtub, the water swirling around her. He froze, his breath catching in his throat. Lily turned, her platinum hair plastered to her forehead, her eyes wide with surprise. "Josh!"

she exclaimed, her voice a soft gasp. He stammered, mortified. "I… I'm so sorry, Lily. I didn't realize… I just needed a towel, and…" He turned to flee, his cheeks burning with shame. "I'll just… I'll get one from the hallway closet." "Josh, wait," she said, her voice softer now.

He hesitated, his back still turned. "I really am sorry," he mumbled. "I didn't mean to intrude." "It's okay," she said. "Really. You didn't do anything wrong." He slowly turned back, his eyes fixed on the floor. "I shouldn't have just barged in like that." Lily shifted in the water, a small smile playing on her lips. "Josh, look at me," she said gently.

He raised his head, his gaze meeting hers. He couldn't help but notice the water droplets clinging to her skin, the soft curve of her shoulder, the way the light danced in her eyes. He felt his heart pounding, a mixture of embarrassment and something else – something akin to awe. "You don't need to be ashamed or embarrassed," Lily said, her voice calm and reassuring. "Aren't you my husband." He frowned. "I know, but…" "And," she continued, her eyes sparkling, "I'm yours, Josh. You know that, right? My body is yours to do with as you please. To admire, to touch, to… play with." She paused, her smile widening. "Isn't that how it is?"

Josh's eyes widened. He knew that David's wives had a unique relationship, and the dynamic was very interesting. He knew his place as a husband. But to hear Lily so candidly express herself like this, it was something else entirely. "Did… did you learn that from your stepmothers?" he asked, his voice fighting against his embarrassment. Lily nodded. "They've taught me a lot. About love, about duty, about…

160

submission." She tilted her head, her expression curious. "Doesn't that please you, Josh? To know that I belong to you completely?"

He swallowed hard, his mind racing. He had never considered himself a dominant man, but there was something undeniably intoxicating about Lily's words, about her willingness to surrender herself to him. He thought about how he always admired David's charisma and confidence, yet he viewed that as a standard he could never attain. But hearing Lily encourage him to be exactly that seemed to unlock something deep within.

He took a step closer to the tub, his eyes fixed on Lily. "I... I don't know what to say," he admitted. "Say you want to join me," she said, her voice teasing. "Say you want to admire me." He hesitated for a moment longer, then a slow smile spread across his face. He understood now. This wasn't about him being inadequate or unworthy. This was about trust, about intimacy, about the unique bond they were forging. "You're right," he said, his voice gaining confidence. "I shouldn't be ashamed. You are mine, Lily."

He reached for the buttons of his shirt, his eyes never leaving hers. "And I think," he continued, a playful look in his eyes, "that I do want to join you." He peeled off his shirt, tossing it carelessly onto the floor. He reached for his belt buckle, undoing it with deliberate slowness. "But first," he said, a playful smirk on his face, "stand up. I want to see you. I want to admire every inch of your beautiful body."

Lily's eyes widened, a blush creeping up her neck. She slowly rose from the water, the droplets cascading down her skin like liquid diamonds. She stood before him, completely unashamed, completely vulnerable, completely his. "Yes, sir," she whispered, her voice trembling slightly. Josh felt a surge of power course through him, a power he had never known he possessed. He stepped closer, his gaze sweeping over her from head to toe, taking in every curve, every detail. "You are magnificent," he breathed, his voice thick with emotion.

Lily leaned back against the porcelain, her eyes half-closed, a small smile playing on her lips. Her platinum curls were plastered to her forehead, framing a face that, in this moment, was both innocent and utterly knowing. He reached for her, pulling her gently against him. Her skin was slick and smooth, and the contact sent a shiver down his spine. He wrapped his arms around her waist, his hands tracing the curve of her back. "You feel good," he whispered, his lips brushing against her ear. "I feel...powerful," she breathed, her fingers tangling in his hair. "Like I could conquer the world."

He chuckled, a low rumble in his chest. "Maybe we will." In this godforsaken new world, anything felt possible. He kissed her then, a deep, lingering kiss that stole her breath away. He felt her respond, her body melting against his, her arms tightening around his neck. The water swirled around them, a silent witness to their burgeoning passion. He deepened the kiss, his tongue tracing the seam of her lips, urging her to open. She complied, and he tasted the sweetness of her, the heat of her desire.

He pulled back slightly, his eyes locking with hers. "Are you sure?" he asked, his voice barely a whisper. Her eyes burned with an answering fire. "More sure than I've ever been of anything." And then, there was no more talking. There was only touch, only sensation, only the rising tide of their desire. He lifted her slightly, her legs wrapping around his waist. He felt her gasp, a small, involuntary sound that ignited a new wave of need within him.

He began to move inside of her, slowly at first, then with increasing urgency. The water splashed, the sounds echoing in the small bathroom. He felt her grip tighten, her nails digging into his back. He heard her moans, soft and breathy, and they drove him wild. He pushed harder, deeper, until he felt her body clench around him. He cried out, his own release washing over him in a wave of pure ecstasy.

They stood there for a long moment, tangled together, their breath coming in ragged gasps. The water cooled around them, but the heat between them lingered. Finally, he eased them both down, sinking back into the water, holding her close. He rested his chin on her head, his heart pounding in his chest. "How do you feel?" he asked, his voice still hoarse. Lily shifted in his arms, a playful look returning to her eyes. "Like a gorilla on cocaine," she said, a grin spreading across her face.

Josh burst out laughing, the sound echoing in the small room. "A gorilla on cocaine?" he repeated, shaking his head. "That's... quite the description." She shrugged, nuzzling against his neck. "Accurate, though. You make me feel...unhinged. In the best way possible." He held her tighter. "And how do I make you feel?" she asked. He sighed contentedly. "Like...like my life has a purpose. I know that sounds cheesy, but it's true. Before, I was just…drifting. Now…now I have you. I have this family. And I have something to fight for." He paused, a sudden thought striking him. "You're my secret weapon, Lily. You know that, right?" She looked up at him, her eyes shining with love. "That's some big dick energy, Josh."

Chapter 11

It's Child Endangerment

As per David's request, his children, little David, Brian, Lily, and Grace were on the shooting range, instructing the others on various hand gun drills. These drills included the failure drill and clearing a malfunction. Little David stood calmly beside Mike, who was currently fidgeting with the Beretta 92FS, looking like he'd rather be anywhere else. Grace mirrored Little David, guiding Bonnie through the same drill.

"Okay, Mike," David said, his voice patient but firm. "Remember tap, rack, bang. If the weapon malfunctions, don't freeze. Tap the magazine, clear the chamber, re-acquire your target, and eliminate the threat." He demonstrated with lightning speed, the pistol barking twice as the targets jerked. Mike nervously mimicked the movements, fumbling slightly with the slide. "Tap… rack… bang," he mumbled, squeezing the trigger. The gun fired, and he jumped slightly. "Damn, this thing kicks!"

Grace, standing a few feet away, chuckled. "You'll get used to it, Mike. Bonnie's already got it down pat." Bonnie, with surprising stoicism for a child her age, was indeed handling the Sig Sauer P365 Macro with surprising grace. She had a wide fingered death grip on the pistol, but she was keeping it on target, squeezing the trigger with a surprising amount of determination. "Tap, rack, bang," she repeated robotically. "Good job, Bonnie," Grace said, a genuine smile on her face.

Nearby, Lily was working with Josh on the 100-yard range. Lily was a natural with firearms. Josh, on the other hand, was trying his best to control the powerful 300 Winchester Magnum rifle. "Okay, Josh, remember what I said about breathing," Lily instructed, her voice calm and steady. "Slow, controlled breaths. Squeeze the trigger, don't pull it."

Josh nodded, adjusting his stance. He took a deep breath, aimed, and squeezed. The rifle roared, kicking against his shoulder. "Josh, my love. If you have to keep adjusting your stance, then you don't have a firm position. It should naturally return to the same site picture after each shot." Josh fired again. "A little high," Lily observed, watching the target. "But your groupings are getting tighter. You're doing great, honey." Josh grinned, relieved. He wanted to impress Lily, and more importantly, David. He knew that earning David's respect was like winning the apocalypse lottery or something.

Back at the 15-yard range, the scene was more... complicated. Seth was standing beside Lynn, Josh's mother. Lynn, however, looked more like a reluctant spectator. "Seth, honey, are you sure this is necessary?" Lynn asked, her voice laced with exasperation. "I really don't need to learn how to shoot." Seth simply tilted his head. "Dad said if you won't learn, then we have to make you watch us practice. It's about situational awareness. Besides, Bonnie and Mike are doing fine, and they're much younger than you." Lynn let out a deep breath. "David just wants his own army of obedient drones," she muttered, earning a sharp glare from Seth. "He's preparing us," Seth corrected. "There are bad people out there, and ignorance is more dangerous than a loaded weapon."

"You know, this is kind of surreal," Andrea said to Jill, as she reloaded her magazine. "Two weeks ago, I was dealing with over-emotional patients and egocentric doctors at the hospital. Now, I'm learning failure drills from a kid who probably knows more about guns than most people I've ever met."

Jill chuckled. "Tell me about it. Parker was a bit rusty when we started, but now he's back in form. It's like we've been transported back to the wild west, but with better weaponry and worse internet." Seo-Yeon was doing well, and with a few modifications, the ergonomics of her pistol were a decent fit for her smaller hands. David junior himself, customized her personal sidearm.

In the main house's bunker, Taylor, Kayla and Nicole were helping Jennifer expand the hydroponics garden, which would now consume 5,200 square feet. Aidan and Alissa were making a list of materials they would need for their 'Vehicular Rampage' project. Tiffany was doing yoga with Tanya, Jessica and Elena in the recreation bunker. David was in the work shed with Kyle. "So, these are the weapons you got the other day?" Kyle asked, looking through the assorted semi auto rifles and pistols. "Yeah, just let me know if there's something unique about these," David said.

"Alright, let's start with these AR-15s," Kyle said, picking up one of the rifles. "Standard M4 platform. Nothing special here, but clean and well-maintained. These pistols, though..." he picked up a Glock 19 and examined it closely. "These have aftermarket triggers, and the slides have been milled for a red dot, plus some stippling work. Someone put some love into these."

David nodded. "I figured as much. That actually tells me a lot." Kyle stopped, setting the pistol down. "What does it tell you?" he asked. David picked up one of the AR-15s. "These rifles are the same manufacturer, which means they were purchased by a business, otherwise the accessories would be all over the place. Plus the Glocks, these aren't some hand me down law enforcement or military side arm. I'm thinking personal security."

Kyle chuckled. "Give me time. I'll strip them down and see if anything else interesting pops up. I'm more curious about the supplies you're planning to gather on these runs. Are you sure it's worth the risk?" "Positive," David replied, his eyes focused on a list he'd gotten from Aidan. "We're going on the offensive. And honestly," he paused, looking at Kyle, "we need to know who we're up against.

Letting them dictate our movements is a bad strategy." "So, a calculated risk," Kyle said, understanding dawning on his face. "Use the supply runs to bait them out. See what kind of force we're dealing with." "Exactly," David confirmed. "I'm not going to send anyone into a death trap. We'll scout ahead, our routes, and be prepared for anything. But sitting here waiting for them to come to us... that's just asking for trouble."

Later that afternoon, David addressed the group. "I'm planning a series of supply runs over the next few weeks," he began, his voice calm and steady. "We need to gather more resources, expand our training, and most importantly, understand the threat we face."

He outlined the potential targets: He wanted to acquire material for armoring his remaining vehicles, and possibly another truck. As far as ammunition, he knew he had enough, but he also knew that reloading supplies and more ammunition meant more training. He detailed the risks involved, the possible encounters with other survivors, and the potential for conflict.

The aroma of Tiffany's pot roast, mingled with Summer's rosemary-infused mashed potatoes, filled the large living room. David, standing before his assembled family, radiated an energy that bordered on unsettling. "We're going shopping," David announced, his voice carrying over the sizzle of the cooking. Jessica, nestled comfortably in his lap, giggled. "Shopping, Daddy? For what? Designer shoes and vintage artwork?" She punctuated her question with a playful squeeze of his thigh. Tanya, perched behind him on the sofa, leaned forward to nibble at his ear. "Perhaps some gourmet coffee, Sir? You deserve it after all you do for us."

Lynn, observing from the periphery, wrinkled her nose. The public displays of affection were... excessive. And the way David spoke about potentially getting everyone killed while his wives fawned over him? It was like tasteless satire. David, unfazed by the combined assaults on his senses, continued. "Not paintings, Jess. Not coffee, Tanya. We're going shopping for armored plating, maybe a new truck, and enough ammo to make Rambo feel emasculated."

Aidan, leaning against the French door, straightened. "You think someone will shoot at us?" "Someone did shoot at us, if you recall," David corrected, his gaze hardening. "And while I appreciate saving on ammunition, I prefer not to be on the receiving end of unprovoked lead poisoning." Brian chimed in, "The surplus depot on Highway 6? Plenty of trucks, lots of sheet metal. Should be a good place." Seo-Yeon nodded in agreement, her fingers carefully slipping into his pockets.

Summer, simultaneously stirring a pot with one hand and scribbling notes on a pad with the other, said, "I'll map out potential routes, catalog known threats, and calculate fuel consumption. "Excellent," David approved. "Taylor, Kayla, I'll need you both to assist Summer with her preparations. Elena, I want you to help Brian with creating a distraction plan, in case we are ambushed."

Elena, her eyes sparkling with mischief, grinned. "Distraction? Oh, Sir, I do love a good distraction." Nicole spoke gently, "David, are you sure this is necessary? We have plenty of supplies. Is it worth the risk?" David's expression softened as he looked at Nicole. "It's not about what we need, Nicole. It's about what we learn. We can sit here, wait for the world to come to us, and become complacent targets. Or, we can go out there, observe, learn their tactics, and show them that we are not to be trifled with. This trip isn't strictly necessary, you're right, but it will be fun."

Jennifer, a mischievous look in her eyes, piped up. "Sounds like fun, Master. Can I drive?" David chuckled. "You can drive, Jennifer. But you're not allowed to run anyone over. Unless they started it." Lily, squeezed next to Josh on the couch, discreetly slipped her hand down his pants. Josh, normally stoic, subtly tensed. He cleared his throat. "I… I'll go with you, David. Me and Lily can handle security." "Perfect," David smirked.

Lynn, finally unable to contain herself, blurted out, "But… but why? Why risk yourselves? Why put yourselves in danger? You have a baby on the way, David! And all of you…" She gestured at the wives, a mixture of bewilderment and disapproval etched on her face. "You're all just… nodding along! Are you not worried?"

David fixed Lynn with a steady gaze. "Worry is a luxury we can't afford, Lynn. Fear is a tool to be controlled, not a master to be obeyed. And as for Jessica… well she can stay here. Jessica frowned and batted her eyelashes at David. "Oh, Daddy, please can I come? The baby will be safe." "No, Jess. You are not coming. I want you here." "I suppose I can stay here and do all the cooking while you have all the fun," Tiffany said with a playful huff, crossing her arms over her chest. "Please, Tiffany, I need you here this time. But I promise to take you next time," David said calmly.

Seth raised his hand. "I want to take security on the convoy," he said. Grace nodding beside him. Lynn's face crumpled. "Oh, no, no, no! Absolutely not! You can't be serious! A child? Going out there with guns? David, this is insane! It's reckless! It's… it's child endangerment! You can't let him do this!" She was sputtering now, her voice rising in pitch with each word. She couldn't believe what she was hearing, this child was going to play mercenary.

David listened patiently to Lynn's escalating tirade, his expression unreadable. He knew her anxieties stemmed from a place of fear and a fundamental misunderstanding of their reality. He turned to Tiffany, his gaze direct and unwavering. "Tiffany darling, could you please get me a kitchen knife? A good, sharp one." Tiffany, unfazed by the bizarre request, calmly rose from her seat and disappeared into the kitchen. She returned moments later, a gleaming knife held out to David.

David took the knife, the metal cool against his palm. He turned back to Lynn, his voice calm and measured. "Lynn, you seem very concerned about Seth's safety. You think it's reckless and irresponsible to let a child go out on such a dangerous 'field trip,' as you so eloquently put it." He paused, letting his words hang in the air. "Tell me, Lynn, do you honestly believe you could do a better job protecting this community than Seth?"

Lynn, momentarily caught off guard by the direct question, stammered, "Well, I... I... I don't know anything about... you know... fighting and stuff. But I'm an adult! I'm more responsible!" As Lynn continued her monologue about how reckless and irresponsible it was to let a child go out on such a dangerous "Field trip", David's movements were lightning fast. He threw the knife at Seth with full force.

The knife spun through the air, a silver blur against the backdrop of the living room. Lynn gasped, her eyes widening in horror as she saw the weapon hurtling toward the unsuspecting child. She opened her mouth to scream, but the sound died in her throat. Seth, without a flicker of emotion, without even blinking, reached out and snatched the knife from the air, his fingers closing around the handle as if it were being handed to him. The knife stopped dead, inches from his chest. He examined the knife, his expression thoughtful, then turned and gave David a barely perceptible nod.

Lynn stood frozen, her face pale, her eyes wide with disbelief. The air hung thick with stunned silence. David smiled, a genuine, affectionate smile. "See, Lynn? Seth can handle it. Now, are there any other questions? " The rest of the room burst into laughter, except Lynn, who proceeded to faint on the floor.

The sound of Lynn collapsing onto the floor was a muffled thud amidst the lingering chuckles. Jessica gave David a playful shove. "Show off," she whispered, a smirk dancing on her lips. "But I'll admit, it was pretty impressive, Daddy." She winked, earning a grateful purr from Luci.

Parker, Eric, and Scott, along with their respective families, were a variety of stunned expressions. They'd witnessed David and his children's... eccentricities before, but the knife-throwing stunt had taken the cake. Jill was the first to break the spell. "Okay, well," she said, clearing her throat, "that was certainly... memorable. Moving on, what's the actual plan for the convoy?"

Mike, oblivious to the undercurrent of shocked intrigue amongst the adults, bounded toward Seth, his eyes wide with admiration. "Dude, that was freaking awesome! You're the coolest friend I've ever had!" Seth, unfazed by the praise, simply shrugged, a ghost of a smile playing on his lips. "I'll teach you how," he said as he casually tossed the knife back to David, the glint of the blade catching the light before David caught it. David, in turn, handed it back to Tiffany, who, with the air of a seasoned professional, wiped it clean and returned it to its place in the kitchen.

As Tiffany walked back to the living room, Jennifer sidled up to Jill, a predatory gleam in her eye. "Oh honey," she purred, her voice low and suggestive, "I am so going to suck his dick so hard for that." Jill's eyes widened as she struggled to suppress a snort of laughter. Meanwhile, David clapped his hands together, drawing everyone's attention back to the matter at hand. "Alright, folks, back to business. Aidan will lead the convoy, his co-driver will be Elena. Seth, you're with Aidan. Jennifer, You're driving the van, and I'll be with you. Lily and Josh, you're security for the second vehicle. Parker and Eric, I want you riding with us."

"Now, about Lynn," Summer interjected, glancing at the still-unconscious figure on the floor. "Perhaps we should move her to one of the guest rooms in the bunker. And maybe a stiff drink when she wakes up." "Already on it," Kayla said, smoothly guiding Parker and Scott towards Lynn. "Need a hand?" They hoisted Lynn up, her limbs limp and unresponsive, and began carrying her towards the stairs leading down to the bunker.

As they disappeared down the stairs, Jessica leaned against David, her hand resting on her belly. "You know," she said softly, "sometimes I worry about what kind of world this baby is going to be born into." David wrapped an arm around her, pulling her close. "It will be a challenging world, Jess," he admitted, his voice low. "But, lets also try to make the most of it."

As Lynn disappeared down the stairs, Alissa leaned toward Aidan. "Can you do that? Catch a knife like that?" she asked, squeezing his arm. "Mmhmm, we all can," he answered dismissively. "Most of our childhood was hand-eye coordination drills. Dad even made them into games." Alissa thought a moment. "But why take the risk?" Aidan squeezed her hand. "The consequences were dire, sure, but with training, the probability was nearly zero. Plus, the way dad threw the knife, if it had hit Seth, it would have struck him with the handle."

Meanwhile, Lily was still playfully fondling Josh inside his pants, giggling softly. His face turning a particular shade of red as he tried to pay attention. "Daddy, Brian said Highway 6, does that mean we're going to Houston?" Lily asked, unconcerned with Josh's current state of embarrassment. "Looks like it, Lily-bug. I'd like to stop by La-Porte anyway. I want to grab some ultra-high molecular weight polyethylene." Jill furrowed her eyebrows. "How much of that ultra-high cellular weight... that stuff you mentioned, how much do you need?" David smiled. "I want to get as much ultra-high molecular weight polyethylene as possible."

Jessica rolled her eyes. "Why don't you just abbreviate it, or call it Dyneema? Do you have to enunciate the whole name every time?" David straightened his back. "You see, ultra-high molecular weight polyethylene is the product, Dyneema is a product name, more than the product itself.

And besides, I like saying ultra-high molecular weight polyethylene more," he said confidently. Brian and Elena, now in on the joke, decided to join in on the harassment. "David, what do you plan on using the ultra-high molecular weight polyethylene for? Are you going to make cutting boards?" Elena asked, a smug smile on her face.

David shook his head. "No Elena, that's high density polyethylene. Ultra-high molecular weight polyethylene is a thermoplastic polyethylene with an extremely high molecular weight. Which results in exceptional toughness, abrasion resistance, and a low coefficient of friction." Brian raised his hand. "So dad, are we going to use the ultra-high molecular weight polyethylene as armor?" David nodded his head. "Yes Brian, we can use ultra-high molecular weight polyethylene to make a lot of things, and armor is right at the top of the list." Jessica, who's eyeballs were about to roll out of her skull, sat up. "Ha, ha, ha. You people are fucking hilarious."

As Scott and Parker returned from the garage, they felt a strange mix of annoyance and sadistic humor emanating from the group in the living room. "What did we miss?" Parker asked. Jill, now wearing an amused expression, looked at her husband. "David wants to get materials to make armor." "Oh, like Kevlar?" he asked, settling back into his seat. "No, David was talking about… what's it called again?" Jill asked, looking to David. "Oh, you mean ultra-high molecular weight polyethylene?" Jessica, now completely frustrated, stood up. "Fuck you guys," she said, walking into the kitchen.

As David concluded the meeting, Lily took Josh by the hand to their room. She wasn't about to waste the opportunity to spend quality time with her husband. Meanwhile, dinner was served. "You guys are more than welcome to join us, but the table is full, so we'll have to eat in here," David said, gesturing around the room. Brian and little David immediately assessed the situation and ran off, returning with two long folding tables and several folding chairs. David, after seeing his boys react to the situation, offered a firm bump of the fists.

Back in the dining room, Bonnie surreptitiously observed Seth. The image of him, cool and collected, snatching that knife out of the air, replayed in her mind. It was an act of impossible skill, an undeniable display of strength and control. A thrill she wasn't expecting, went through her. Before she knew it, she found herself sneaking glances at him, mesmerized by his every move. As Seth and Mike were talking about something Bonnie had absolutely no interest in... a question fell out of her mouth. "Seth, do you have to watch Miss Lynn again tomorrow?" Her cheeks flushed a rosy pink, and she avoided eye contact with everyone except Seth, who, ever the polite young man, raised an eyebrow in polite inquiry. "Well," Bonnie continued, stammering slightly. "I just thought, you know, different instructors offer different perspectives. Maybe I could work with you on the shooting range tomorrow instead? A broader outcome, right?"

David paused mid-bite, his autism tingling. He processed the information: Bonnie's sudden interest in Seth,

Grace's barely veiled annoyance, and the underlying implication of Lynn's potential... inconvenience. He cataloged it all for later analysis. Jessica, perched beside him, nudged him playfully. "See, Daddy? Even in the apocalypse, teenagers are still teenagers. Although, I gotta admit," she leaned in, "the knife thing was kinda cool. But seriously, can we please talk about something other than ultra-high molecular weight polyethylene for five minutes? My brain is starting to feel like it's made of... well, you know." David chuckled. "Duly noted, Baby."

Jennifer, however, was far from laughing. The image of David's controlled aggression, the flash of steel, the sheer dominance he exuded when he threw that knife... it had created an itch, and she needed David to scratch it, immediately. She subtly kicked his leg under the table, earning a brief, quizzical glance from Summer across from her. "Master," she purred, her voice dripping with unsubtle invitation. "Could you come help me with something in the hydroponics? I think I saw something... concerning."

David blinked. Something concerning? In hydroponics? While not entirely implausible given the current state of affairs, it seemed highly unlikely. He internally cross-referenced Jennifer's tone, body language, and past behavior. Conclusion: "Something concerning" was code for " desperate, immediate fornication."

He sighed internally. He did love Jennifer's... enthusiasm. But her timing was inconvenient, and their hydroponics garden was a masterclass in gardening without soil. "I'm rather occupied at the moment, Jennifer. Perhaps

Brian could assist you with the... hydroponics issue?" Jennifer practically vibrated with frustration. "Brian? Really, Master? He wouldn't be able to fix it like you could!" She shot Brian a glare, who merely shrugged, accustomed to being dismissed as a non-expert in the "art of seduction."

Meanwhile, Lily and Josh re-entered the dining room, radiating a post-coital glow that was hard to miss. Lily immediately sought out David. "Daddy," she said, snuggling against his arm. "Josh was amazing at the range today! He's getting so good with the 300 Win Mag. It was so hot." She blushed slightly, but the look in her eye betrayed her true meaning. Josh, now emboldened by his recent... performance and, let's be honest, Lily's uninhibited enthusiasm, stood a little taller.

Bonnie, emboldened by Lily's anecdote, piped up again. "So, Seth? About tomorrow," she began, twirling a strand of her hair. "Maybe after you're done with Miss Lynn, we could... I have some questions about reloading techniques." Seth, ever oblivious to the burgeoning romantic interest, nodded enthusiastically. "Sure! I can show you everything I know. We can even try some different powder charges. Dad's got a ton of reloading equipment in the work shed." Bonnie's face lit up. A date at the reloading bench with Seth? Post-apocalyptic romance was certainly unconventional, but she was all in.

David surveyed the scene, his mind already racing with a thousand calculations. The convoy, the security protocols, the potential threats beyond the valley, the... hydroponics. And now, the burgeoning teenage drama. He cleared his throat, his attention turning back to the logistical nightmare that was the convoy. "Now, as I was saying about the ultra-high molecular weight polyethylene..." Jessica groaned, burying her face in her hands. "Oh, for crying out loud..."

Chapter 12

A Stark Realization

As the aroma of bacon and eggs filled the air, David sat at the dining room table watching his family work. Summer and Kayla were on breakfast duty, a chore that seemed to feel like a part time job, considering the sheer number of people to feed. Jessica, nauseous from her pregnancy was quietly sitting, as Tanya brushed her hair and applied light makeup. Tiffany was comparing the ranch schedule with the security patrol schedule as Elena watched, sipping her coffee from her seat. Jennifer, however, was bed ridden. She had tempted David after dinner, and he made sure she got what she longed for.

Taylor and Nicole were in the process of setting up a classroom in one of the guest bedrooms, downstairs in the garage. Even though Seth and Grace really had no need for a conventional education, they were not the only children, and education was just as important as training.

Downstairs, Aidan and Seo-Yeon made breakfast in the kitchen as Lily, Josh, Alissa and Brian prepared for the days training and activities. Meanwhile, David was setting the table in the downstairs dining room. Inside Parker's apartment, he and Jill monitored the camera feeds from the comfort of their living room through their LCD windows, a feature they grew to appreciate, especially with how things were going outside.

Lynn, having recovered from yesterday's incident was starting to realize that she was way out of her league. David seemed to have an answer for everything, and his children certainly didn't need her protection and intervention. As she flipped through the various feeds on her own window, she noticed Scott and Andrea in the work shed, talking with Kyle over a pile of semiautomatic rifles and pistols. Maybe she should go see what they were talking about.

After making her way upstairs to the work shed, Jill greeted her with a polite nod. "So David wants to integrate these into his arsenal?" Scott asked, gesturing toward the weapons on the table. "Yeah, so far his own weapons have been loaned out and we've already examined these as much as we can." Kyle said, reassembling the last of the pistols. Lynn stepped forward, wanting to understand David's intent. "So, what's going to happen to these guns?" Lynn asked, placing her hands on one of the rifles. "They're going to be issued to everyone, especially those that didn't bring a weapon."

Kyle pulled out a list. "We have thirteen rifles and Glocks, which is enough to arm everyone here, with more to spare." Lynn considered her position in the family. She had been an inconvenient guest. Tolerated because of her son's relationship to David's daughter. If she wanted to understand this world, she was going to have to become part of it. "Kyle, do you think you can show me how to use these? I want to learn too." Kyle smiled, a knowing look on his face. "Let's start with the Glock. The first thing to remember, is that there is no safety selector switch on it..."

Back at the main house, Aidan and Seth had set up a game of catch. Aidan, Seth, Grace, Brian and Lily were on one side, with Mike, Bonnie, Josh, Seo-Yeon and Alissa on the other. Casually at first, they tossed rubber knives back and forth, progressively increasing the speed and distance. This was the game David developed, which was just a small part of his training plan. His children, who were already more than proficient in handling edged weapons, worked patiently with their partners. Even if they never held a knife again, the confidence they would gain in themselves would be a greater benefit than any trick or skill with a knife.

Back in the main house, Jennifer padded into the dining room, still feeling slightly disoriented. The afterglow of David's... atomic dong, still lingered, both physically and mentally. She glanced around the table. Tiffany was meticulously labeling containers of leftover bacon grease. Summer was meticulously wiping down the counter. Kayla was meticulously calibrating the coffee grinder. Tanya was meticulously flossing her teeth. Elena was meticulously washing dishes. And Jessica was meticulously trying not to throw up.

David, finished with his breakfast, stood up and clapped his hands together. "Alright, everyone, let's get to work! Jennifer, the school room needs to be tidied up. Mike and Bonnie need a proper learning environment, and I already have Nicole and Taylor starting that." Jennifer blinked. "School room?" "Yes," David said, his expression patient.

183

"We need to ensure the children receive a proper education, even in these... unconventional circumstances."

Elena piped up. "And who's on security detail today, oh wise one? Surely you're not expecting those overgrown toddlers to handle everything." David smiled. "Parker is monitoring the perimeter using the hidden cameras. Much less conspicuous than having armed guards patrolling the grounds. Besides," he added, winking at Elena, "I have complete faith in my children's abilities."

Just then, Lynn walked into the dining room. She was wearing a pistol belt, and a Glock was strapped to her hip. The room went silent. Forks clattered against plates. Jessica nearly lost her breakfast again. "Lynn?" Tiffany asked, her voice laced with cautious surprise. Lynn, her face flushed but her eyes determined, held up her hands. "Relax, everyone. The magazine is full of dummy rounds. I'm just... getting used to carrying it." A long silence followed, broken only by the purring of Lucipurr, who was curled up on Jessica's lap.

Lynn cleared her throat. "I... I wanted to apologize," she said, her voice trembling slightly. "I know I've been overbearing, untrusting. It's just... hard for me to adapt." She looked directly at David, her eyes pleading for understanding. "But I'm ready to start contributing. Really contributing." David studied her for a moment. Then, a flicker of approval crossed his face. "Kyle is going to take me to the shooting range later, to get used to firing a gun." She explained. "That's good news," David said. "In the meantime, continue practicing today until you no longer have reactive interference," he added.

David patiently explained, "Reactive interference is when your body tenses up before pulling the trigger, causing you to miss your target. It's important to stay relaxed and focused when handling a firearm. You'd be surprised how many new shooters hit the target on the first try, then spend the rest of the time shooting off the paper. That's why." Lynn nodded, understanding the concept. She took her seat at the table, still feeling a bit out of place amongst the group. David sensed her discomfort and decided to break the ice.

"Lynn, I'm glad you're taking the initiative to learn how to use a firearm," David said, smiling warmly at her. "It's important for everyone to know how to protect themselves and their loved ones in these times." Lynn felt a surge of gratitude towards David. She had always seen him as a dominant and capable figure, but she never realized how genuinely caring he was. She made a mental note to herself, to be more open and trusting towards him and his family.

The clatter of silverware against plates, usually a comforting sound in the fortress-like dining room, felt amplified to Lynn's ears this morning. Every scrape, every clink seemed to echo the tremor of anxiety still humming beneath her skin. She chewed on the last bite of the surprisingly delicious, scrambled eggs (thank goodness for chickens), watching Elena efficiently scrub dishes, and Summer wipe down the already spotless kitchen counters. Jennifer had excused herself with a quiet "I'm going to help in the schoolroom," a simple statement that carried the weight of newfound purpose and, Lynn had to admit, impressed her immensely. He didn't forget about school.

Lynn swiveled in her chair. "Okay, I need to ask something. It's been bugging me." Elena, never one to mince words, turned, a dishrag dangling from her hand. "Oh, here we go." Lynn ignored the comment. "David…how did he know? How did he know to be so prepared? This house, the bunkers…it's not just a coincidence, is it? And he talks like he knows things are going to get worse. How?"

A beat of silence hung in the air. Elena rolled her eyes, clearly not wanting to engage. Tiffany, Tanya and Summer exchanged glances. There was a silent conversation passing between them, a weighing of options. Finally, Tiffany, ever the diplomat, spoke. "Lynn, the world ending, as you know it, already happened. I think you are now one of us, and it's probably time you know." Summer chimed in. "It's not exactly a secret anymore, now that we're all…living it." She gestured to everything around her. "Okay…" Lynn said, her eyes searching theirs, "tell me."

Tanya started first. "David…experienced something. Something impossible. He…" She hesitated, searching for the right words. "He regressed," Tiffany stated simply, "back to 1993. From this same apocalypse." Lynn stared, her jaw slack. "Regressed? You mean…time travel? Like in a movie?" Summer chuckled humorlessly. "Think less 'Back to the Future,' more 'unexplained phenomenon that allowed him to retain all his memories and knowledge from the future. I mean, he was just a kid when he woke up in the past." "So, everything he's done, everything he knows…it's because he's lived through this already?" Lynn asked, the pieces slowly clicking into place. "That's how he knew to build this place, how he knew about the EMP, about the blackout…" Tiffany nodded. "That's why he's so…prepared. And why he's so confident in his decisions." Lynn ran a hand through her hair, her mind reeling. "But that's…insane. How is that even possible?"

Elena finally speaks up, "You're asking the right question, but there is no answer." "And the kids…" Lynn voiced her next question, a new wave of bewilderment washing over her. "Aidan, Brian, Lily… they are all incredible, like prodigies. They know things they shouldn't. They…" Summer finished her thought, "They also carry his memories and knowledge," Summer said. "Not all of it, but…enough. Enough to make them incredibly capable." "That's why they're so…self-sufficient," Lynn realized, thinking of Josh and Lily. She's still trying to fully trust Lily with her son. "That's why they're always training. He's preparing them, preparing all of us, for what he knows is coming." Tanya nodded. "Exactly."

Lynn absorbed the information, the sheer improbability of it all battling with the undeniable evidence before her. It explained so much – David's unwavering certainty, his almost preternatural ability to anticipate problems, the unsettling calm that radiated from him even during the chaos of the past two weeks. "So, what's next?" Lynn asked, a new determination solidifying within her. "If he knows what's coming, what are we going to do?" Tiffany smiled, a genuine, reassuring smile. "We follow his lead. We learn, we prepare, we survive. Together."

Elena, surprisingly, offered a rare almost smile. "And try not to ask too many stupid questions. We've only got one David, and he's got enough on his plate." Lynn chuckled, a genuine laugh that eased some of the tension in her shoulders. "Fair enough. But one more question...Does he ever talk about what it was like? The first time around, I mean?" Tiffany sighed. "That's where the notebooks come in." "Notebooks?" Lynn asked, confused. "He wrote everything down. Thousands of pages," Tanya said. "His experiences, his observations, his strategies." "We've all read them. Multiple times, actually. It's kind of required reading around here." Summer added. "We know what he went through. He was alone, Lynn. Losing his faith, losing his humanity. Just surviving, waiting for death to claim him."

Lynn's heart ached at the image of David, alone and lost in a ravaged world. "But... weren't you with him? Then?" The three women exchanged a look, a silent communication passing between them. Tiffany shook her head slowly. "No, Lynn. None of us were." Lynn's eyebrows shot up. "But... how? He's... he's so good at... well, at everything! You'd think a man like that would have a whole army of people around him, even before... all this." She gestured vaguely, encompassing the apocalypse outside.

A knowing look passed between the women. Tiffany stood up, "Come on, Lynn. Let's go somewhere a bit more comfortable." She led the way, Summer, Elena, Kayla, and Tanya trailing behind, into one of the living rooms. Tiffany went directly to a large bookshelf, her hand hovering over a thick, leather-bound volume. With a grunt, she pulled it free.

"This," Tiffany declared, holding the book aloft, "is David. Or, at least, a part of him."

Lynn reached out tentatively, running her fingers across the embossed title. "What is it? A diary?" "More like a…journal, his account," Elena said, a playful smirk on her face. "Think of it as the Cliff's Notes to the end of the world, according to David, apocalypse edition." Lynn sat on the edge of one of the sofas, her eyes wide. Tiffany settled beside her, opening the book carefully. Elena and Tiffany bit their lip. "What the hell is this?" Lynn scoffed. Collectively, the entire group erupted into laughter. "I'm sorry Lynn, David made up an enigmatic code to keep prying eyes from this information. We all know it, so we don't even see it anymore," Tiffany explained.

Lynn began flipping through the pages. "David started writing this almost immediately after…he came back," Summer explained gently. "He needed to get it all down, just in case his memories faded. It's…intense. It's how we know what to expect, and how to prepare." Kayla leaned forward. "It's not just about practical stuff, though. It's about him. His thought process, his feelings…everything. You have to understand, Lynn, David…sees the world differently. He processes information in a way most of us can't even comprehend. It's part of what makes him…him." "And what makes our children so…adept," Summer added softly. "They have that same…analytical mind. But they also have David's experience, ingrained in them subconsciously. It's like they were born with a cheat code for survival."

Lynn shook her head, still struggling. "But... how could he have been alone? Surely, he had family, friends... someone to share this with?" Summer sighed, a shadow passing over her face. "That's... a long and painful story. He started alone. He was alone when the blackout hit. He had a life before us, a different life. A life he desperately tried to save." "A life he failed to save," Elena interjected, her voice sharp, though devoid of malice. She leaned against the doorframe, a mischievous glint in her dark eyes. "That failure is what fuels him. It's what made him the man he is today."

Tiffany reached over and gently squeezed Elena's hand. "Not failed, Lena. He learned. He adapted. He built something better. Something... safe." Summer continued, her voice softening. "Before us, he had three sons. Grown up. After the blackout, his first instinct was to find them. But..." She paused, her voice catching. "They were... gone. Killed. And their families. His ex-wife..." She trailed off, shaking her head. "She refused to let them bring their weapons inside. Said it was too dangerous." A wave of nausea washed over Lynn. She could imagine the horror, the helplessness. Her own son, Josh, flashed through her mind. "Oh, God," she whispered.

Tanya put a comforting hand on Lynn's shoulder. "It gets worse, I'm afraid. After his divorce, he had a series of disappointing relationships, which only hardened him more. But someone broke through, he called her his true love. Someone he loved very much. Samantha." Elena picked up the narrative, a hint of steel in her voice. "His true love, as he calls her. The one that got away the first time around. He went to find her too, after losing his sons. But she was already dead."

Lynn gasped. The weight of David's past, the sheer magnitude of his loss, threatened to suffocate her. "He carried that with him for seven years," Kayla said, her voice low. "Seven years of scavenging, fighting, surviving in a world gone mad. All alone. Seven years of reliving the deaths of his sons, the loss of Samantha." "And yet," Tiffany added, a fierce pride in her voice, "He still built this." She gestured around the kitchen, the house, the ranch, the entire fortified compound. "He still lives with that trauma, and yet despite it all, he saved us, all of us."

Elena smirked, a playful glint returning to her eyes. "He built a harem, more like it." She winked at Lynn. "But hey, who's complaining? We're all pretty happy here." The tension in the room eased slightly, replaced by a nervous chuckle from Lynn. "A... harem?" Summer laughed, a genuine, lighthearted sound. "Technically, yes. But it's not how it looks. It's... complicated. We're a family. We support each other. We love each other. And we all love David, in our own way." "He probably looks like a scumbag, hoarding all the women, but that's not the case." Kayla added. "We basically threw ourselves at him, and none of us knew about his plan until after we committed to him, to his family... his community."

Tiffany nodded in agreement. "He's... different. He sees the world in a way that most of us can't. But he uses that to protect us, to guide us. He's a leader, a provider, a protector. And he's also..." She blushed slightly. "Incredibly affectionate." "And he's got that whole Dominant thing going on, which… well, some of us appreciate," Elena added with a wink, earning a playful shove from Tanya.

Lynn, acquiesced. "Right. Well, he certainly seems to have a hold on all of you." She paused, a thought striking her. "I can't believe that someone divorced him." The words were out before she could stop them. A sudden silence descended onto the room. Tiffany's smile faltered. Summer and Kayla froze. Elena's leg stopped swinging. Tanya stopped drinking mid gulp. "That's… not something we talk about," Tiffany said finally, her voice carefully neutral. "Yeah, that's ancient history," Summer added, a flicker of something unreadable in her eyes. "Let's just say… certain mistakes were made, and lessons were learned," Elena said with a cryptic smile.

Lynn, sensing she'd stumbled onto forbidden territory, quickly changed the subject. "So, how did you all meet him? I'm just… curious." Tiffany relaxed visibly, grateful for the change of subject. "I met him… well, technically, I've always known him. We were neighbors. I moved across the street when I was sixteen." She smiled, a dreamy look in her eyes. "He was… different then. Still David, but… younger, less weathered. But even then, there was this… maturity, this wisdom about him. Irresistible, really." Lynn's jaw dropped slightly. "Wait, you were sixteen and he was… how old?" "Fourteen," Tiffany said, matter-of-factly. Lynn choked on her own saliva. "Fourteen?! You fell in love with a fourteen-year-old boy?"

Tiffany nodded her head. "Yeah. I was going to be a junior, and he was just starting his freshman year, but even

192

then, he had this... presence. This quiet confidence. I was completely infatuated." "And you, a sixteen-year-old, started chasing after a fourteen-year-old boy?" Lynn asked, her voice incredulous. Tiffany laughed. "You have no idea. I tried everything. I flirted, I wore provocative outfits, I even tried to get him alone a few times. But he just kept rejecting me. He'd be polite, even friendly, but he never took the bait. It was infuriating!" "He knew what she wanted. But he wouldn't let her do anything until he was sixteen." Summer said, laughing. "I tried to seduce him?!" Tiffany scoffed with a grin. "I did! I thought he was a prude, but he wasn't. He was just waiting. Said it wasn't right, and I admit, I liked that he thought that way, even if it was infuriating"

"I've known him since I was nine," Summer said, her gaze faraway. "We kinda grew up together. He was just David then – a quirky, quiet kid. But when he... changed," she hesitated, searching for the right word, "when he regressed, it was like a switch flipped. I knew something was different." "That's when you got interested?" Lynn asked, her eyes wide. Summer nodded. "Yeah. He was still David, but he was... more. More aware, more confident, more... everything. When I was sixteen, I started finding excuses to be around him. I took art classes, changed my schedule, even asked him to tutor me."

Elena smirked. "See, Lynn? Everyone has a story. Mine's a bit more...complicated." She paused, a shadow crossing her face. "I was married to an immature loser when I met David. And David was already...well, David was already juggling Tiffany, Jennifer and Summer. I met them when David and I were in Language school. In his past life, he was still married, so he kept our relationship professional." "This time around though," Tiffany, off to get the tea kettle going, interjected, "We basically recruited her." "Basically, I was friends with Tiffany, Jennifer and Summer. But David...motivated me in a weird way." Elena continued. She shrugged. "I ended up staying with them for nearly a year before I fell in love with David." "You had no exit strategy," Lynn asked. "Exactly. But," Elena wrapped an arm around Summer and Tiffany, "It was the best decision I ever made."

Kayla leaned in slowly. "I met David in Arizona. I'm one of the ones that had dreams about him. Vivid dreams, like remembering a past life... because it was." She paused, gathering her thoughts. "Apparently, in David's past life, before he met Samantha, we were... seeing each other. It was... intense. The intimacy... I felt so unloved by my husband back then, so I was seeing David on the side." Her voice trailed off, tinged with regret. "After I got pregnant, I decided to try and stay with my husband. Turns out, he'd been banging his ex-wife, and I completely overlooked it last time. I chose wrong. I know it now. That's why I dreamt of David. I was remembering our past life... and I truly loved him."

Tanya shifted uncomfortably, a wave of embarrassment washing over her face. "Well, my story is less... romantic," she mumbled, avoiding eye contact. "I didn't have any dreams. I just... felt him. From the moment I met him." She hesitated, then continued, "It was in Seattle, a few years ago. He just felt so... familiar. Like I'd known him my whole life. Turns out," Tanya said, her voice barely audible, "we did meet. Or, at least, we did in his past life. He met me right before his regression, so he had never gone back at that point. In his past life, I was in a really bad place. The world had broken me, physically, emotionally, psychologically. David... he showed me kindness. He fed me when I was starving, he protected me from the dangers of the world... and because I was beyond repair and suffering terribly, he ended my life to end my pain."

A hush fell over the room. The women stared at Tanya, their faces a mixture of shock and sympathy. "This time," Tanya continued, her voice stronger now, "he found me before that happened. He sought me out because he knew what I'd end up going through." Lynn frowned, piecing together the puzzle. "But how did he find you, if the world was already gone when you met?"

Kayla answered, "Apparently he was living in the Pacific Northwest at the time, with his brother and mother. He said when he met her, under the scars, he noticed her tattoos." Kayla added, "When David's mom, Teresa, was sick, we went up there. Then David and I went looking for her. That's when we found her and brought her back here." Lynn's brow furrowed. "So, David remembered Tanya's tattoos from a chance meeting before his regression, knowing he would need that information to find her again in a future life? That's... incredibly specific."

Kayla shook her head. "I don't think David knew he was going to look for her, he certainly wouldn't have known then. But he remembers everything from his past life with perfect clarity." Summer nodded. "In Tanya's case, that was beneficial. But he also has nightmares. His past still haunts him. Luckily, most of his trauma has been resolved." Lynn was intrigued, "Resolved how?" Tiffany interjected, a warm smile gracing her lips. "He needs us, Lynn. Our trust, our… presence. It keeps the chaos in his mind at bay." She paused, choosing her words carefully. "David will move heaven and earth to take care of us, as long as we let him. As long as we allow him to be our bedrock. Apparently, he lacked that in his past life, hence the loneliness."

Lynn mulled over this information. She could understand how David's rigid structure, his meticulous planning, and his unwavering dedication provided a sense of grounding for him. Saving Tanya beforehand, preventing the tragic events of his past life, was certainly a proactive way of dealing with trauma. And Kayla. Reconciling with her, before she settled on her loser husband. "But what about… Samantha, his lost love?" Lynn asked, her brow furrowed. "The one he couldn't save. Couldn't he save her?"

At that moment, Jessica sauntered into the living room, looking much better than an hour ago. She was humming a jaunty tune, her hand resting protectively on her slightly rounded stomach. She caught the tail end of the conversation. "That was me, I'm Samantha," she said casually, as if responding to roll call. She plopped down on the floor, cross-legged, and scratched Lucipurr behind the ears.

A stunned silence descended upon the room. Lynn's jaw practically hit the floor. Tiffany, Summer, Elena, Kayla, and Tanya exchanged knowing glances, a slight smile growing on their lips. Like David, they enjoyed these revealing moments.

Lynn sputtered, "You... you're Samantha?" Jessica giggled, a sweet, youthful sound. "Well, I would have been. When I was nineteen. Before... everything. It was a name I chose to protect myself. But none of that happened this time. This time, I got Daddy." She gave a playful wink. Lynn blinked, the cogs in her brain visibly whirring. "But... how?" Jessica stretched, an impossibly graceful movement in her current condition. "I've been dreaming about David since I was thirteen. It was like... gravity. Like a black hole. Pulling me towards him. I felt like I knew everything about him. I even regained all my memories of him the night we had sex for the first time." Jessica's eyes danced with mischief. "It was quite the memorable experience." "Right," Lynn said weakly, gripping her mug tightly.

Chapter 13

An Ex-Wife's Revelation

David... regressed? Like, Benjamin Button, but with apocalypse sprinkles on top? The idea was so outlandish, so utterly bonkers, that it short-circuited her already anxious brain. And the ex-wife! Letting their children die because she was scared of guns when she was married to... the David? The David who could probably bitch slap a rifle round out of the air, mid-flight? It was all too much. Kyle sighed, gently correcting her grip on the Glock 19. "Lynn, you're squeezing too tight. Relax. Imagine you're holding a baby bird... a very, very angry baby bird that could peck your eye out."

Lynn managed a weak smile. "Right. Baby bird. Got it." She lifted the pistol, closed one eye, and promptly flinched as she squeezed the trigger. The bullet sailed wildly off-target, kicking up dust a good five feet to the left. "Okay," Kyle said, his voice carefully neutral. "Let's try that again. Remember, slow and steady..." "How could anyone divorce him?" Lynn blurted out, interrupting Kyle's instructions.

Kyle blinked, clearly taken aback. "Uh... divorce who?" "David!" Lynn exclaimed, throwing her free hand up in exasperation. "I mean, okay, he's... pragmatic. And maybe a little weird. But he's caring. In his own end-of-the-world, hyper-competent, ridiculously overprotective way. How could someone just walk away from that?" Kyle shrugged, carefully avoiding eye contact. "People have their reasons,

Lynn. Maybe pragmatism wasn't her love language?" Lynn scowled. "It's not fair! I just hope that woman's miserable right now."

Before Kyle could respond, a familiar voice called out, "Having trouble hitting the broad side of a barn, Mom?" Josh strolled onto the range, Lily trailing behind him, carrying her SIG Sauer P365 Macro. Josh had his P226 holstered at his side, his expression a mix of amusement and genuine concern for Lynn's well-being. Lily offered a warm smile. "Don't worry, Lynn. It takes practice. And patience."

Lynn deflated. "I just don't get it. According to these women, he was all alone, and now, I feel like I am intruding even now." Josh stepped forward, his young face hardening with a touch of David's characteristic intensity. "David's not alone now, mom. We're all here for him. And that includes you." Kyle nodded in agreement. "Yeah, Lynn. You're part of the family now. And we look out for each other."

Lynn felt a lump form in her throat. Despite her initial reservations about David's... unconventional family dynamic, she was starting to feel a sense of belonging she hadn't experienced in... well... ever. "Okay," she said, taking a deep breath. "Let's try this again. Show me that baby bird grip." Kyle grinned. "That's the spirit!" He readjusted her stance, guiding her hand with gentle precision. Josh offered tips on breathing and focusing, his advice surprisingly insightful for someone his age. Lily simply stood beside her, her presence a quiet source of encouragement.

Lynn concentrated, pushing aside the swirling thoughts about David's past and the looming apocalypse. She focused on the target, the feel of the gun in her hand, the slow, steady squeeze of the trigger. Bang! The bullet hit the target, closer this time. Not a bullseye, but a definite improvement. "See?" Lily said, clapping her on the shoulder. "You're getting there!"

Emboldened, Josh decided to show off a little. He raised his P226, aimed deliberately, and fired off a magazine. The shots were all clustered tightly around the center of the target. Lynn smiled. "Nice shooting, Josh!" Lily, always eager to demonstrate her superior skills, grabbed her P365 Macro. With a blur of motion, she drew the weapon, aimed, and fired. Bang, bang, bang, bang, bang, bang, bang, bang, bang, bang, bang, bang, bang, bang!

Fourteen holes appeared in the target, all within a three-inch circle. Before anyone could fully process what they'd just witnessed, Lily spotted a jackrabbit darting across the field. Without hesitating, she raised her pistol again and fired a single shot. The rabbit dropped instantly. A stunned silence fell over the range. Lynn's jaw hung open. Josh stared at Lily with a mixture of awe and disbelief. Even Kyle looked impressed.

Lily shrugged, her expression nonchalant. "Just practicing. Gotta keep my skills sharp, you know? Plus, never waste a day at the range." After kissing Josh, she walked over to retrieve her kill. Lynn recovered first, bursting into laughter. "Okay, okay, I get it! You're all terrifyingly competent. I guess I have a lot to learn." "Remember, Lynn," Kyle said, his voice calm and steady, "squeeze the trigger, don't yank it. Smooth and steady."

Lynn, to her credit, was improving. Her shots were no longer veering wildly into the neighboring county; most were now at least kissing the edges of the paper target. Josh, as expected, was much better. His shots were all hitting the target, a testament to the rigorous training he'd received. Lily, on the other hand, was less interested in paper targets and more focused on eradicating any unfortunate rodent or reptile that dared to venture into the open fields. "Got one!" she chirped, sighting in on a distant rattler. "That's a snake!" she said, marking her bingo card. David would be proud.

"Alright, Mom, keep practicing," Josh said, turning to face her. "You're getting there. By next week, you'll be hitting center mass like a pro." He paused, reloading his pistol. "Hey, did… did you hear this from David?" Lynn blinked, lowering her weapon. "Well, not directly. But… Tiffany, Summer, Kayla, Tanya, and Elena filled me in after breakfast. It was like an intervention, but instead of alcohol, it was… alternate timelines." Josh winced. "Yeah, that sounds about right."

Lynn shuddered. "The Jessica thing… that was particularly unsettling. To think, he lost the love of his life, and now she's here! And pregnant! It's like some bizarre time-travel romance novel. The one with the amnesiac hero." "And the part about Tanya?" Josh prodded gently, steeling himself.

Lynn's face paled. "Oh god, don't remind me! I thought I was losing my mind. The fact that David… that he killed her… out of mercy… but still. And that she loves him more for it in this one… I just don't know what to make of it." Josh nodded, a melancholic smile playing on his lips. "Tell me about it. I heard the unabridged version, and I was

201

freaking out for days when I heard it. It's a lot to process, huh?" He knew, better than anyone, that "freaking out" was an understatement. The sheer weight of the information, the implications of David's regressed memories, the sheer improbability of it all... it had been a mental marathon.

Lynn sighed, wiping sweat from her brow. "Unsettling is one word. Tragic, definitely. But... I'll be okay. I think." She paused, a flicker of curiosity in her eyes. "I heard most of it... but they didn't talk about how he met Nicole, Taylor, or Jennifer. Though, I imagine it's more of the same. Except the whole ex-wife thing." Josh's eyes widened slightly. He didn't know she would take it so well. "So, mom, how did you react when you found out you were his ex-wife?"

Lynn froze. The last shot ringing off to God knows where. She stared at Josh, her mouth stuck open, eyes wide with a mixture of terror and disbelief. "Ex-wife? Me?" she stammered, her voice suddenly broken. Kyle glanced over, a concerned expression on his face. Lily, oblivious to the unfolding drama, continued her hunt for rogue rodents, a determined glint in her eye.

Josh's stomach dropped like a lead weight as he watched his mother's face crumple. He hadn't meant to drop that bomb, hell, he assumed Tiffany and the others had spilled every detail during their chat. But now, seeing Lynn's wide-eyed stare, her mouth hanging open like a faulty gate, he realized his epic blunder. "Mom, I... uh, wait, that came out wrong," he stammered, his voice cracking like a teenager caught sneaking out. Great, just great. Way to go, Josh.

Announce family secrets at the shooting range like it's casual chit-chat over coffee.

Lynn stood frozen, the Glock 19 still clutched in her hand, but her grip had gone slack. The gun wobbled precariously, pointing at nothing in particular, which made Josh's heart race even faster. He lunged forward, gently prying it from her fingers before she accidentally turned the range into a catastrophic slapstick comedy sketch. "Whoa, Mom, let's not add 'accidental discharge' to today's highlights," he said, forcing a chuckle that sounded more like a nervous squirrel. In his mind, he was already replaying the conversation: How could he have been so dense?

Kyle, ever the steady hand, paused his coaching stance and glanced over with a furrowed brow. He was mid-demonstration on proper sight alignment, but now his focus shifted to the unfolding drama. "Everything okay over there?" he asked, his voice laced with concern. "Lynn, you look like you've seen a ghost."

Lily, meanwhile, was off to the side, blissfully unaware at first. She crouched near the edge of the range, her pistol holstered as she scanned the overgrown grass for those pesky rodents. But when Lynn's sharp intake of breath cut through the air like a bad punchline, Lily straightened up, brushing dirt from her knees. "What's going on? Did someone finally admit they're terrible at shooting?" She grinned, but her expression shifted when she saw Lynn's pale face. "Oh. That doesn't look good."

Josh swallowed hard, his mind racing. He could feel the heat rising in his cheeks. It was supposed to be a simple afternoon—training, bonding, maybe a laugh or two about the world's end. Instead, Josh had just detonated a verbal grenade. "Mom, listen, I didn't mean to just blurt it out. I thought you knew. About... you know, being his ex-wife in that other life."

Lynn blinked, finally finding her voice, though it came out in a high-pitched squeak that could have been straight out of a sitcom. "Ex-wife? Me? As in, the one who left him and... and caused all that tragedy?" She pressed a hand to her forehead, swaying slightly as if the weight of the revelation might topple her. "Oh, for the love of... Josh, you can't just say things like that! I mean, I just learned about David's whole time-jump thing from the girls, and now this? It's like finding out you're the villain in your own rom-com rewrite." She let out a breathless laugh, but it was edged with hysteria, her eyes darting between Josh and Kyle as if searching for a lifeline.

Kyle stepped in with a deadpan expression that could cut glass. "Wait, hold up. David's ex-wife? Like, the one from his stories? The one who... yikes." He whistled low, shaking his head. "Man, that's a plot twist I didn't see coming. No wonder you're freaked, Lynn. But hey, in this timeline, you're not that person. You're just... you. Overbearing mom extraordinaire." He shot Josh a sideways glance, trying to lighten the mood, but Josh could see the gears turning in Kyle's head.

Lily holstered her gun and approached, her steps light and purposeful. "Okay, seriously, what did I miss? One minute we're blasting targets, the next Lynn looks like she's about to faint." She looped an arm through Lynn's, guiding her to a nearby bench. "Come on, sit down before you pull a comedy routine and face-plant into the dirt. And Josh, what the heck did you say?"

Josh groaned inwardly, sinking onto the bench beside them. From his limited perspective, this whole scene felt like a bad improv skit he'd been dragged into. "I just... I just asked how she handled finding out she was his ex-wife. I thought Tiffany and the others told you everything when they explained his regression."

Lynn sank onto the bench, fanning herself with her hand as if that would ward off the absurdity. "Well, they didn't! They talked about his loneliness, how cruel I... I mean, she... was for leaving him and letting everything fall apart. But they didn't say it was me! Me!" She let out a laugh that bordered on manic, her voice rising in pitch. "I mean, can you imagine? In some alternate universe, I'm the one who breaks David's heart, and now here I am, living on his ranch like it's a post-apocalyptic family reunion. It's like a bad rom-com where the ex shows up for the sequel."

Kyle chuckled despite himself, crossing his arms. "Hey, at least you're not alone in the weirdness department. What's one more plot twist? Besides, from what I've heard, David's not holding grudges. He's all about second chances, hence the whole harem setup." He winked, trying to inject some humor, but Josh shot him a glare. Not the time, dude.

Lily, sensing the tension, jumped in with her playful energy. "Okay, but think about it this way, Lynn. In this life, you're not that ex-wife. You're Josh's mom, and you're here, safe, with us. Plus, David's warming up to you, right? That's progress! And if anything, it means you two have some cosmic chemistry. Who knows? Maybe you'll end up as his... I don't know, bonus wife or something." She giggled, earning a horrified look from Lynn.

"Lily! Oh, heavens no. I'm already dealing with one overbearing parent label; I don't need to add 'accidental polygamist' to it." Lynn managed a weak smile, the color slowly returning to her cheeks. "But seriously, Josh, you scared the life out of me. Next time, lead with something less... earth-shattering. Like, 'Hey, Mom, want to hear about the time David fought off raiders with a car antenna?'"

Josh let out a relieved laugh, the knot in his chest loosening. "Fair point. Sorry, Mom. I guess I'm still getting used to all this myself. David's stories are wild, but living them? That's a whole other level." He glanced around at the group, the shooting range now feeling less like a training ground and more like a confessional booth. Lynn reached over and squeezed Josh's hand. "Alright, enough drama. Let's get back to shooting before those rodents think they've won. But if anyone else has secrets, save them for after coffee. Deal?" "Deal," Josh replied, his heart lighter.

Hours later, in David's room, Lily barged in. "Dad, you won't believe it," Lily said, her voice a mix of playful exasperation and genuine concern. Lily's words tumbled out like a poorly aimed scattershot. "So, Josh blurts out that Lynn was your ex-wife, and she just... freezes. Like, mid-Glock hold. Kyle's trying to play it cool with his deadpan jokes, but Lynn... was fanning herself like she was in a bad rom-com. She looked like she might faint or shoot something by accident. It was hilarious, but also, y'know, not." Lily plopped onto the bed as she waited for his reaction. David wasn't mad at Josh, he understood slip ups.

He knew how Lynn thought; meticulous, overbearing, a helicopter parent through and through. Now, here she was, entangled in his extended family, and the poor woman was probably spiraling. "Alright, Lil," he said, his voice steady but laced with his signature wit. "Sounds like we need to turn this into a comedy sketch, not a tragedy. Grab Josh; we're going to talk to her. And remember, no more secrets on the range, that's the rule now."

Lily grinned, looping an arm through his as they headed out. Josh was waiting in the hallway, looking like a farm boy who'd just been caught stealing cookies. "Dad... er, David, I swear, I thought she knew," Josh stammered, his voice cracking. David clapped him on the back, not missing a beat. "Relax, kid. If I got mad every time someone spilled a family secret, we'd be out of coffee by now. Let's go fix this."

They made their way out to the work shed, and down the stairs to Lynn's apartment door. David knocked lightly. "Lynn? It's David. And Josh. We're not here to stage an intervention... yet." From inside, he heard a clatter, followed by a string of muffled curses. She was probably still practicing disassembling and reassembling her Glock. David felt a pang of understanding; he knew her anxiety stemmed from guilt and disbelief.

The door swung open, revealing Lynn in a state of disarray. Her hair was tied back haphazardly, and she clutched the Glock like it was a life raft. "David, I... I don't know what to say. This is ridiculous. Me? Your ex-wife? I mean, in what universe does that make sense?" She fanned herself dramatically, her helicopter-parent energy on full display. Josh shifted uncomfortably beside David, whispering, "See? This is why I should've led with coffee."

David stepped inside, motioning for Josh to close the door. The apartment was neat, if a bit cluttered with family photos. David sat on the edge of a couch. "Lynn, breathe. I know you're overwhelmed. Hell, I was too when I first jumped back. But let's cut the drama, it's not like we're in a soap opera. You were my ex the first time I went through this, sure, but that's neither here nor there. I'm not holding grudges; and we're both learning from our past."

Lynn set the Glock down, her hands trembling slightly. "But I really left you and it led to... tragedy. I feel guilty, David. Like I'm the villain in your story." She laughed nervously, but it came out more like a hiccup. David placed his hand on hers. "We were simply incompatible. You were incapable of trust, and I was too weak to control you." Suddenly, Lynn saw a chance at redemption. "What if this is all a mistake? What if I'm not really her?" she asked, a look of hope in her eyes.

David let out a deep breath. "Lynn, you have a tattoo on your ankle that your cousin gave you in church. You were chased by the neighbor's dogs when you were a young girl…" David spent the next thirty minutes revealing Lynn's deepest darkest secrets from her childhood, a diarrhea of information that left Lynn feeling completely defeated.

David watched Lynn's face cycle through a whirlwind of emotions; shock, relief, and that exhausted resignation that made her seem like a side character who'd just discovered her script was rewritten. She slumped into the chair opposite him, her hands finally releasing the Glock as if it were a hot potato. "So... what do we do now?" she asked. David shook his head. "Nothing changes." "Nothing changes?" she echoed, her voice a mix of disbelief and cautious hope. "I'm just Josh's mom, part of this... weird, fortified family reunion?"

"Exactly," he said, his voice steady but laced with that dry wit that always disarmed people. "In this life, you're not my ex-wife. You're Josh's overprotective mom, and frankly, that's a full-time job. We don't have room for grudges when we've got other things to worry about." Lynn fanned herself again, her haphazard bun coming undone in dramatic fashion. "But David, I mean, what if I screw it up again? Am I supposed to just... blend in? Play nice in your little compound?" She gestured vaguely toward the ceiling, as if the layers of bunkers above them were a personal affront.

David leaned back, crossing his arms with that commanding presence that had drawn so many to him. He couldn't help but smirk. "Lynn, if blending in means you stop treating Josh like he's five and start helping with the ranch, we're golden. Remember, this isn't ten years ago. Things are different now, and we have some sense of normalcy to maintain."

As David left, Josh remained standing by the door. He watched his mom, Lynn, sink into the worn armchair, her face flushing a shade of crimson that could rival the sunset. She'd just had what Josh could only describe as a 'eureka moment gone wrong,' a sudden, awkward epiphany about her and David. In David's regressed timeline, they had... well, had sex. And David, surely, remembered every detail.

Josh stifled a snort, leaning against the doorframe with his arms crossed. At his age, he was no stranger to awkward family conversations, but this? This was prime comedy material. "Wait, so you're just now piecing this together, Mom? Like, out of nowhere?" he asked, his voice dripping with amusement. Lynn fanned herself with a dog-eared magazine. "Josh, don't you dare laugh! This is... this is mortifying! I mean, what if he thinks about it every time we talk? Oh God, does he?" She buried her face in her hands, peeking out between her fingers.

Josh couldn't hold it in anymore. A full-bellied laugh erupted from him. "Mom, you're acting like it's a plot twist in a bad soap opera. 'And then, the ex-wife realizes they did the deed in another life!' Classic." He mimed wiping a tear from his eye, his mind already spinning with the absurdity. Here they were, hiding out in a high-tech fortress, and his mom was freaking out over something that never even happened in this timeline. It was almost poetic. "Look, if it makes you feel any better, David's probably too busy bossing everyone around to dwell on it. I mean, the guy's got like nine wives and a ranch to run. You're just a footnote in his epic saga."

Lynn shot him a glare that could freeze boiling water, but it quickly softened into a reluctant chuckle. "A footnote? Oh, honey, in my head, I'm the star of the show. But seriously, what do I even say to him next time? Josh grinned, plopping down on the couch beside her. "You could always ask for details. You know, for science. Bet David's got some stories. He's got that whole dominant vibe going on, remember how he laid out all your childhood secrets? Guy's like a walking encyclopedia of awkwardness."

Lynn swatted at him playfully, her embarrassment fading into a reluctant smile. "You're impossible, Josh. No wonder Lily puts up with you, you've got that same dry wit David has. But fine, let's change the subject before I die of second-hand embarrassment. What's the plan for tonight? More guard duty?" Josh shook his head. "Nah, David told me you could use a break. He wants me to take you to the pool, and Tanya has a spa treatment lined up." Lynn's eyes lit up. She only heard about the pool, but now... now she was going to see it for herself.

David Renado

Tiffany Renado

Jennifer Renado

Summer Renado

Elena Renado

Nicole Renado

Taylor Jones

Jessica Renado

Kayla Brooks

Tanya Jang

Aidan Renado

Alissa Renado

Brian Renado

Seo-Yon Jang

David Jr. Renado

Seth Renado

Lily Renado

Josh

Grace Renado

Kyle

The Red Beast

Lynn